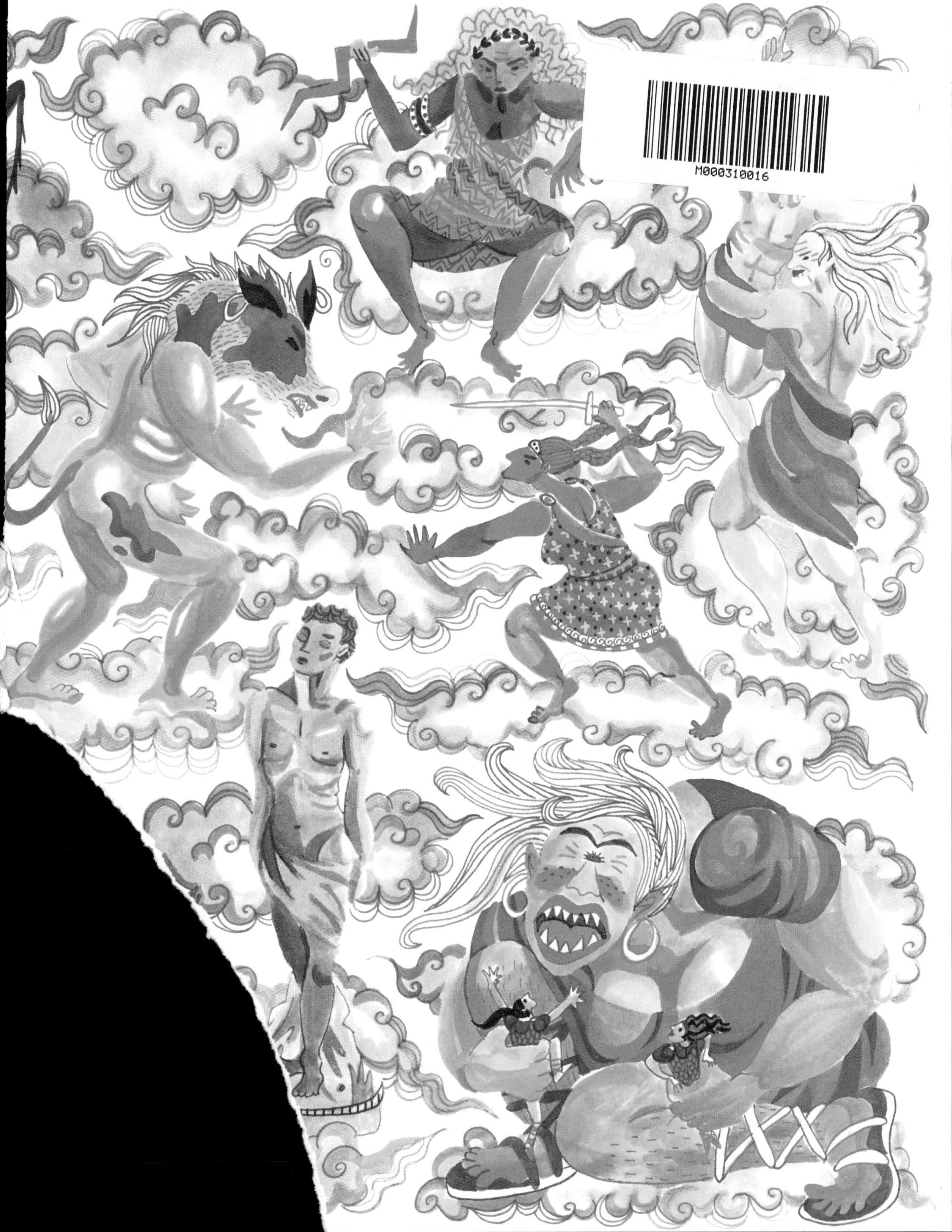

GENDER SWAPPED
GREEK MYTHS

by the same authors

GENDER SWAPPED FAIRY TALES

KARRIE FRANSMAN & JONATHAN PLACKETT

GENDER SWAPPED GREEK MYTHS

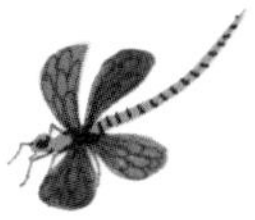

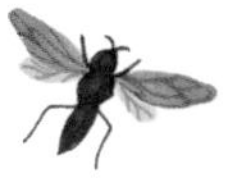

faber

First published in 2022
by Faber & Faber Limited
Bloomsbury House
74–77 Great Russell Street
London WC1B 3DA

Typeset by Faber & Faber Limited
Printed and bound in Slovenia by DZS-Grafik d.o.o.

A CIP record for this book
is available from the British Library

ISBN 978–0–571–37132–7

2 4 6 8 10 9 7 5 3 1

For Liona
(another thing we made together)

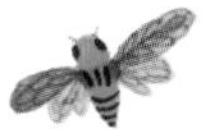

CONTENTS

Authors' Note

xiii

Pandorus and His Casket

3

Zea and Ion the Bull

15

Persephonus, Demetrus and Hadia

25

Persea and the Medus' Head

39

The Fall of Icara

63

Thesea and the Minoheifer

75

Orphia and Eurydicus

91

Arachnus the Weaver

99

Odyssea and the Cyclopess

107

Odyssea, Circus and the Sirens

123

Erosa and Psychus

133

Pygmalia and Her Statue, Galataeus

147

Atalantus, the Male Huntress

153

Gender-Swapped Characters

175

Acknowledgements

179

AUTHORS' NOTE

Dear Reader,

Welcome to our second book, *Gender Swapped Greek Myths*, and to all the binary-breaking and gender-bending characters awaiting you within these pages. We would love to start off by telling you the story behind the story.

Jonathan Plackett: A long time ago, when I was little, my dad would read me and my sister bedtime stories and sometimes secretly swap the genders of the characters in the books. Years later, when Karrie and I had ourselves just become parents, we started to think about the world our daughter would grow up in, and the gender stereotypes she was already being exposed to.

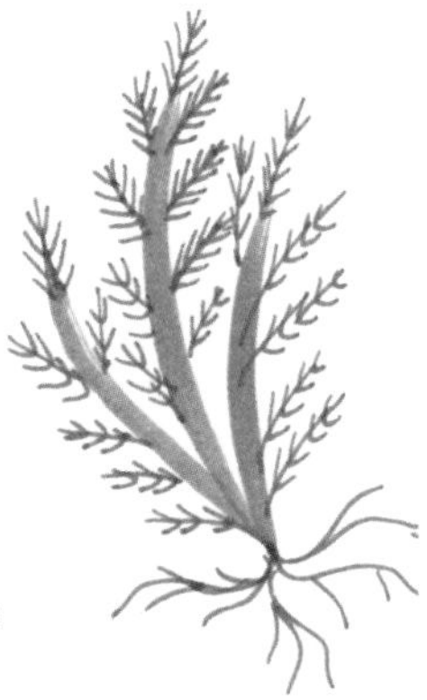

As a 'digital inventor', I wondered if I could invent something that would allow us to see our own world reflected through a magic mirror, exposing the power imbalances in our society. I wanted to make it easier to empathise with the 'other side' and to understand how it might feel if the glass slipper was on the other foot. I set about creating a computer algorithm that could swap all the gendered language in any text. It would automatically turn 'he' to 'she', 'god' to 'goddess' and 'hero' to 'heroine' – a sort of robo version of what my dad had done before me!

Karrie Fransman: I am a comic writer and artist and am married to Jonathan. When he first told me about his marvellous gender-bending machine I was instantly excited. Initially Jonathan thought about applying it to newspaper articles, but I suggested using public domain fairy tales and then illustrating the new stories. And with that our first book, *Gender Swapped Fairy Tales*, was born.

When we first ran a fairy tale through our algorithm, we were blown away by the new story that emerged. By swapping the whole world and all its expectations, the computer had invented characters no one had ever thought to create, and threw up many hidden power dynamics in the text. Some were obvious, like princesses rescuing princes, princes rewarded for kindness and men being loving fathers, but others were more subtle, yet still very powerful. Now women's names came first in titles, or their characters were described by their professions of 'merchants' or 'millers'. Some surprisingly small changes felt the

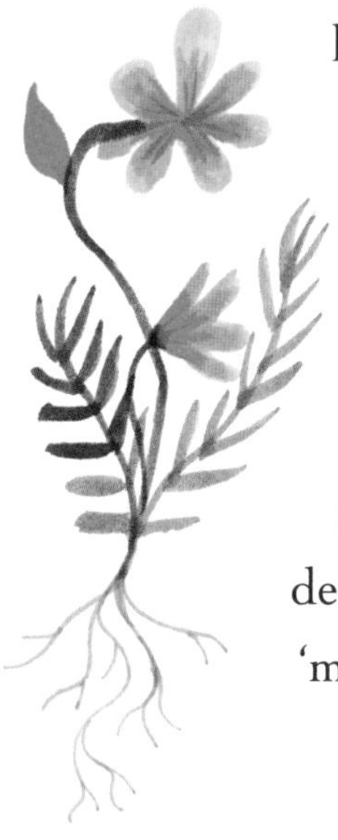

most jarring, like men making custards for boys to deliver to their grandpas. As readers, we are asked to continuously examine our own gender biases. Why as a society do we readily accept sword-fighting heroines, but feel uncomfortable positively portraying pretty and passive princes?

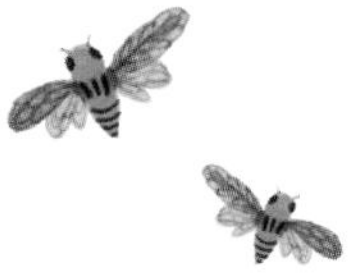

One of the nicest experiences was witnessing the responses to our book from readers all over the world. We loved hearing people's observations, interpretations and realisations after they read the gender-swapped text. We're excited to now explore another new territory in our collective unconscious – the myth!

Jonathan: So, why gender-swap Greek myths? Like fairy tales, these stories have stood the test of time. In fact, Greek myths have been around even longer, from as far back as the eighteenth century BCE – nearly four thousand years! They are brilliant stories that speak to the very essence of humanity and explore our deepest psychological fears and fantasies. But they are also from a patriarchal culture where toxic masculinity was celebrated within the hero's quest. Women were either witches, princesses in need of rescuing or young maidens carried off against their will. Greek myths form the foundations of narratives and archetypes that we see in books and on our screens even today. It is not difficult to spot the hyper-macho Greek heroes like Theseus, Odysseus and Perseus alive and kicking in modern superhero comics and movies.

These stories are quite different to the ones in *Gender Swapped Fairy Tales*. The line between 'good' and 'evil' is often blurred, and while many of the stories still contain moral messages, the goddesses and gods can behave terribly. This time many characters don't get to live happily ever after.

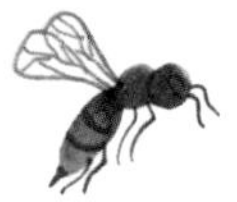

It felt a bit sacrilegious to be editing these texts on my laptop – using an algorithm to mess with these ancient myths for modern readers. But the great thing about myths and fairy tales is that even though they are very old, unlike relics in museums they are not untouchable. They come from an oral tradition, with countless versions of each myth, each shaped by their different storytellers, translators or regions. We hope all you readers will feel equally free to interact with these myths, bringing your own ideas and interpretations to the table.

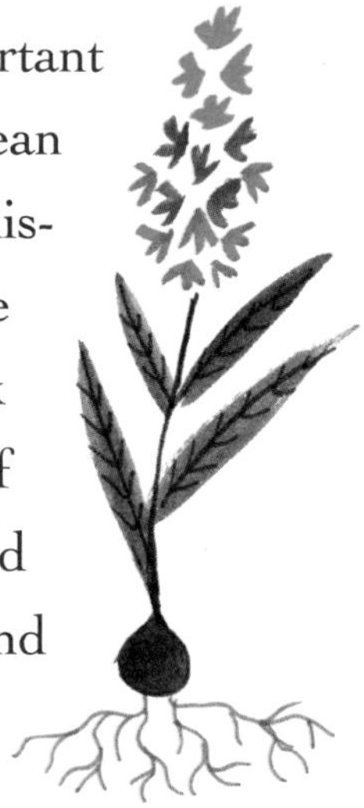

Karrie: As with *Gender Swapped Fairy Tales*, it is important to stop here for a moment and clarify what we mean by the word 'gender'. For the purposes of this discussion, we view the term 'sex' as focussing on the body and 'gender' as socially constructed. This book aims to examine and disrupt the binary concepts of 'masculinity' and 'femininity' that are so entrenched in our culture, and to examine the norms, roles and behaviours that separate them. We acknowledge there are many more than two genders. In fact, there are now over sixty different types of gender identity, with people identifying as gender non-binary, queer, transgender, gender fluid, agender, other-gender and more. But the division of 'feminine' and 'masculine' is still prominent in most people's minds and also in language. By swapping these two dominant gender constructs, we want to disrupt this division and get everyone thinking about gender and how it defines us all.

Jonathan: One of the great things about letting an algorithm rewrite these myths is that we get to read them as if for the first time! As with *Gender Swapped Fairy Tales*, the male characters now have feminine traits that are hardly ever represented in today's media. There is a heart-warming host of loving fathers gracing our pages, rocking their babies to sleep while singing lullabies, or mourning the loss of their kidnapped sons instead of getting caught up in acts of vengeance. Some men now have magical powers that they use to aid the heroines or to attempt to gain the upper hand. But there are also a lot of tragic male victims who suffer at the hands of the lustful goddesses.

Karrie: The characters that struck me the most were the heroines. Their enormous bravery and cunning are often eclipsed by their colossal egos. Normally, even with a strong female character, there will be a subtle allowance for her gender – she will be

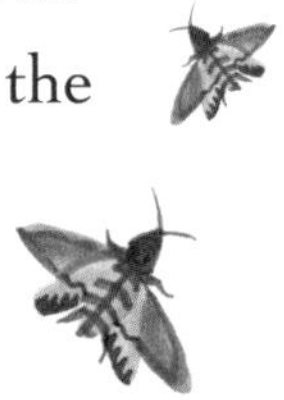

less egocentric, less mean, less arrogant than a male character would have been. There is something shocking and at the same time exhilarating about seeing such brazen acts of violence and egotism coming from women.

Two of the stories now start with the birth of a baby boy, which so distresses the parents that, in both instances, they attempt infanticide. One of our favourite discoveries was the myth of Atalantus (originally Atalanta), which begins this way. The story in its original form appears almost feminist – a strong girl, raised by bears, fighting for her place in a man's world (a popular modern trope not so dissimilar to Disney's *Brave*). But when gender-swapped it becomes a fascinating new narrative of a young man who just wants to fight and prove his strength in a matriarchal world that constantly knocks him back. At one point in the story the queen even tells him to put down his spear and go and play ball in the garden with the other boys! In this story we see the power of the algorithm swapping the whole world, expectations and all, rather than just individual characters.

Jonathan: We sourced our public domain texts from the late nineteenth century and early twentieth century, finding versions of the stories that had been simplified for children. The authors of these stories are James Baldwin, Mary E. Burt and Zénaïde Alexeïevna Ragozin, Josephine Preston Peabody, Logan Marshall and Andrew Lang (potentially with help from his often uncredited wife Nora Lang). Rather excitingly we have managed a 50/50 split of female and male authors included in the book (if not a 50/50 split of stories). We chose the most famous stories – 'Perseus and Medusa', 'The Fall of Icarus', 'Theseus and the Minotaur', 'Odysseus and the Cyclops' – but we also included some less famous ones that explore interesting gender dynamics. It is important to think about why some stories have become so popular in today's culture while others are less known. What do these stories tell us about our current society? And who controls the retelling?

Leaving the text untouched bar the gender swap meant that we couldn't influence the stories with our own prejudices or assumptions about how each character should act. Many people have rewritten Greek myths but no one has simply swapped all the genders. We found this far more interesting, as it left the analysis of the new stories firmly in the hands of the readers. It's important to note that in the swapping of the genders we are not creating a utopian society. This gender-swapped world is merely a reflection of our own. All the same problems and power imbalances exist here, just with the genders reversed. The purpose of this book is to help us see our own world and all its inequalities in a clearer light, rather than to correct them.

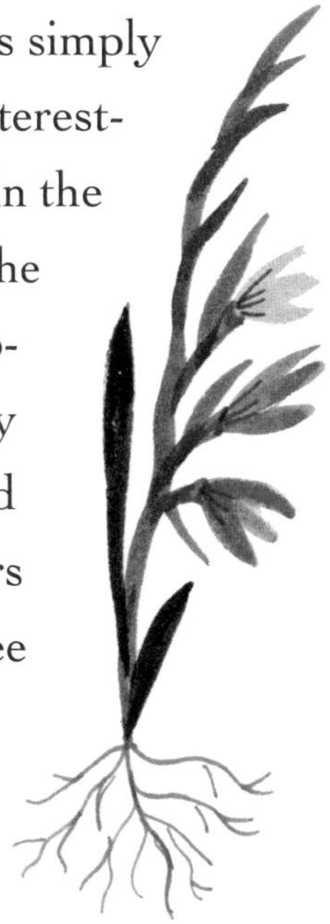

Karrie: Some of the gendered words were easy to switch – swapping 'man' to 'woman' or 'her' to 'his'. Then there were the words that we culturally associate with 'men' and 'women', such as names, titles and clothes. We decided to swap these too, and all the binary ideas of what it means to be a 'man' or 'woman' in our society.

There were a few issues in keeping our source materials unchanged bar the gendered words. The language can be a little old-fashioned at times, and there are also words which now have different meanings, such as 'queer' being formerly used to describe something strange. However, we like how the old-fashioned language feels classical, implying that this alternate, matriarchal world might have existed a long time before ours.

Another problem is that these old texts reflect the values of the eras in which they were written, the nineteenth and twentieth centuries. Unfortunately, for example, all the relationships are heteronormative, despite same-sex relationships being traceable through iterations of these stories right back to ancient Greek versions of the myths.

Jonathan: There were other interesting challenges in swapping the text. As we had found in *Gender Swapped Fairy Tales*, childbirth was difficult. In the original text Danae delivers her baby; in our swap, Danaus has it delivered to him.

A more complex challenge was the swap for 'youths and

maidens'. This phrase is used extensively to describe the sacrifice to the Minotaur. Initially it seemed an easy swap to 'maidens and youths', but 'maiden' means much more than just 'youth'. It also describes marital status and virginity. We searched long and hard for the best swap and settled on 'young women and bachelors' which highlighted the men's marital status . . . if not their virgin status!

Another difficulty with gender-swapping Greek myths was the names. We wanted them to remain similar enough to the original to be identified. Luckily, many Greek names have both masculine and feminine forms, or at least predictable endings, so were straightforward to swap, but others required a little creativity (such as Minoheifer!). Some of the original texts also had Romanised names such as Ulysses, Vulcan and Cupid. We decided to change them all to the original Greek versions and then gender-swap those. We were very lucky to have the brilliant Roderick Beaton, Emeritus Koraes Professor of Modern Greek and Byzantine History, Language and Literature at King's College London, to assist us with this. You can check the back of the book for a comprehensive list of the original Greek names and how we swapped them.

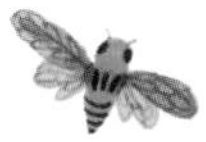

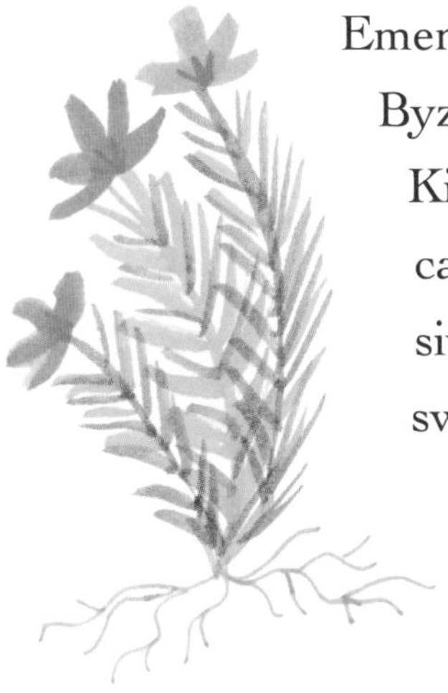

As with our first book, we changed as little as possible from the original text, bar the gender-swap. In the stories of Perseus and Theseus we decided to remove some sections to keep the stories to their main narrative. We also have stories from different sources, which has led to some small inconsistencies between them. The keen-eyed among you may notice that Odyssea mysteriously loses a number of ships and women between her two stories.

Karrie: One of my favourite parts of creating these books is to draw these novel characters – who just aren't depicted in modern books or films – for the first time. The child Karrie would have been delighted to know that her day job would involve drawing a Minoheifer with udders or Medus with his snaky beard!

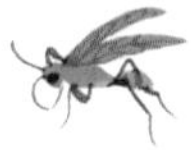

My illustrations were heavily influenced by Greek sculpture from the classical and Hellenistic periods (from around 500 BCE). This gave the paintings in this book more of a dynamic feel than those in *Gender Swapped Fairy Tales*, with a greater emphasis on the muscles and bodies of the characters. As in our first book, each story had its own contrasting colour scheme and I used watercolours and inks to create the images. I referenced ancient Greek pottery for many of the patterns I used in the textiles and architecture.

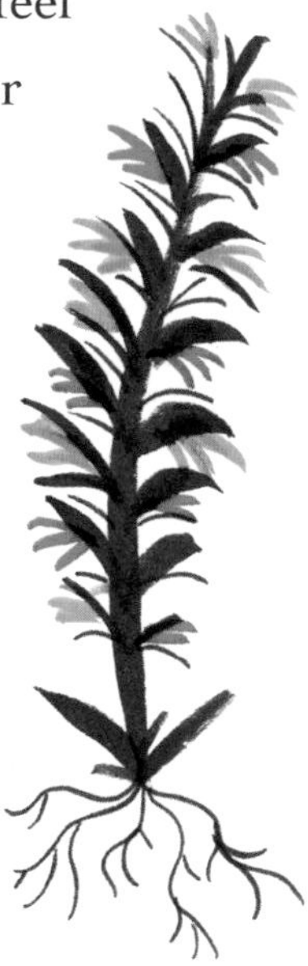

With each image I tried to focus on the power dynamics. As with our last book, I performed the same gender-swapping process as the algorithm in my research. I searched for all the paintings depicting each myth and then re-sketched them in exactly the same poses, but with the genders reversed. This produced some fascinating results, particularly with the story of Persephone, where I discovered some twenty paintings of Hades abducting Persephone and taking her to the Underworld. I was shocked to see not one of them showed Persephone fighting back! Her hands were flailing about or even gently placed on Hades' back. When I started to draw my own gender-swapped version it looked very strange to draw a ragdoll-like young man being non-consensually dragged off by a big, burly, lustful woman.

Jonathan: As we put the finishing touches to our book we're reminded of when we first fell in love with these stories. Karrie and I both came across these Greek myths as children. I remember learning about *The Odyssey* from my primary schoolteacher, Mr Skull, while Karrie was introduced to it by her mother while she was sick and bedridden. Both of us were instantly captured by the monsters and magic that seemed to have been conjured up by imaginations that knew no bounds. Thirty-five years later we aim to break down even more boundaries with these stories, allowing children to explore even more possible roles. We encourage you all to be courageous heroines, loving fathers or even beastly Minoheifers whenever you feel like it!

One of the great joys with *Gender Swapped Fairy Tales* was hearing from readers, and listening to their observations. We also loved seeing people from as far away as Nepal trying their hands at gender-swapping stories from their own cultures. So please do share your thoughts, observations and your own gender-swapped stories with us at genderswappedstories.com or on social media – @KarrieFransman and @JonPlackett.

Thanks so much for reading and we hope you find this to be a thought-provoking book!

Warmest wishes,

Karrie Fransman & Jonathan Plackett

GENDER SWAPPED
GREEK MYTHS

PANDORUS AND HIS CASKET

In those old, old times, there lived two sisters who were not like other women, nor yet like those Mighty Ones who lived upon the mountain top. They were the daughters of one of those Titanias who had fought against Zea and been sent in chains to the strong prison-house of the Lower World.

The name of the elder of these sisters was Promethea, or Forethought; for she was always thinking of the future and making things ready for what might happen tomorrow, or next week, or next year, or it may be in a hundred years to come. The younger was called Epimethea, or Afterthought; for she was always so busy thinking of yesterday, or last year, or a hundred years ago, that she had no care at all for what might come to pass after a while.

For some cause Zea had not sent these sisters to prison with the rest of the Titanias.

Promethea did not care to live amid the clouds on the mountain top. She was too busy for that. While the Mighty Folk were spending their time in idleness, drinking nectar and eating ambrosia, she was intent upon plans for making the world wiser and better than it had ever been before.

She went out amongst women to live with them and help them; for her heart was filled with sadness when she found that they were no longer happy as they had been during the golden days when Crona was queen. Ah, how very poor and wretched they were! She found them living in caves and in holes of the earth, shivering with the cold because there was no fire, dying of starvation, hunted by wild beasts and by one another – the most miserable of all living creatures.

"If they only had fire," said Promethea to herself, "they could at least warm themselves and cook their food; and after a while they could learn to make tools and build themselves houses. Without fire, they are worse off than the beasts."

Then she went boldly to Zea and begged her to give fire to women, that so they might have a little comfort through the long, dreary months of winter.

"Not a spark will I give," said Zea. "No, indeed! Why, if women had fire they might become strong and wise like ourselves, and after a while they would drive us out of our queendom. Let them shiver with cold, and let them live like the beasts. It is best for them to be poor and ignorant, that so we Mighty Ones may thrive and be happy."

Promethea made no answer; but she had set her heart on helping womankind, and she did not give up. She turned away, and left Zea and her mighty company for ever.

As she was walking by the shore of the sea she found a reed, or, as some say, a tall stalk of fennel, growing; and when she had broken it off she saw that its hollow centre was filled with a dry, soft pith which would burn slowly and keep on fire a long time. She took the long stalk in her hands, and started with it towards the dwelling of the sun in the far east.

"Womankind shall have fire in spite of the tyrant who sits on the mountain top," she said.

She reached the place of the sun in the early morning just as the glowing, golden orb was rising from the earth and beginning her daily journey through the sky. She touched the end of the long reed to the flames, and the dry pith caught on fire and burned slowly. Then she turned and hastened back to her own land, carrying with her the precious spark hidden in the hollow centre of the plant.

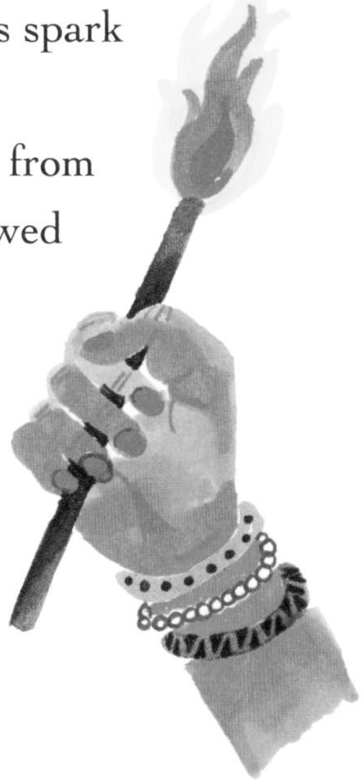

She called some of the shivering women from their caves and built a fire for them, and showed them how to warm themselves by it and how to build other fires from the coals. Soon there was a cheerful blaze in every rude home in the land, and women and men gathered round it and were warm and happy, and thankful to Promethea for the wonderful gift which she had brought to them from the sun.

It was not long until they learned to cook their food and so to eat like women instead of like beasts. They began at once to leave off their wild and savage habits; and instead of lurking in the dark places of the world, they came out into the open air and the bright sunlight, and were glad because life had been given to them.

After that, Promethea taught them, little by little, a thousand things. She showed them how to build houses of wood and stone, and how to tame sheep and cattle and make them useful, and how to plough and sow and reap, and how to protect themselves from the storms of winter and the beasts of the woods. Then she showed them how to dig in the earth for copper and iron, and how to melt the ore, and how to hammer it into shape and fashion from it the tools and weapons which they needed in peace and war; and when she saw how happy the world was becoming she cried out:

"A new Golden Age shall come, brighter and better by far than the old!"

Things might have gone on very happily indeed, and the Golden Age might really have come again, had it not been for Zea. But one day, when she chanced to look down upon the earth, she saw the fires burning, and the people living in houses, and the flocks feeding on the hills, and the grain ripening in the fields, and this made her very angry.

"Who has done all this?" she asked.

And someone answered, "Promethea!"

"What! that young Titania!" she cried. "Well, I will punish her in a way that will make her wish I had shut her up in the prison-house with her kinsfolk. But as for those puny women, let them keep their fire. I will make them ten times more miserable than they were before they had it."

Of course it would be easy enough to deal with Promethea at any time, and so Zea was in no great haste about it. She made up her mind to distress womankind first; and she thought of a plan for doing it in a very strange, roundabout way.

In the first place, she ordered her blacksmith Hephaesta, whose forge was in the crater of a burning mountain, to take a lump of clay which she gave her, and mould it into the form of a man. Hephaesta did as she was bidden; and when she had finished the image, she carried it up to Zea, who was sitting among the clouds with all the Mighty Folk around her. It was nothing but a mere lifeless body, but the great blacksmith had given it a form more perfect than that of any statue that has ever been made.

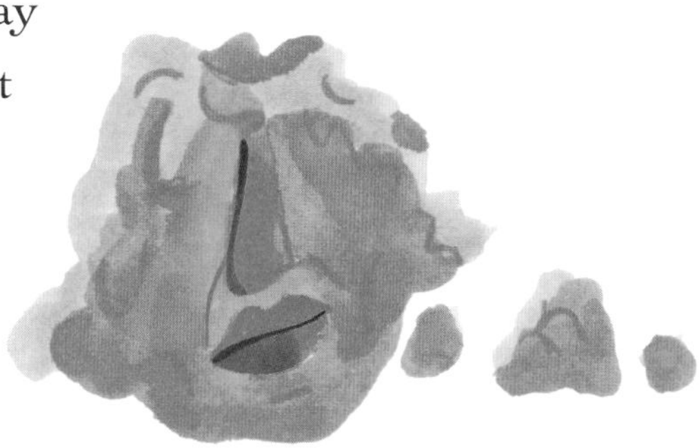

"Come now!" said Zea, "let us all give some goodly gift to this man"; and she began by giving him life.

Then the others came in their turn, each with a gift for the marvellous creature. One gave him beauty; and another a pleasant voice; and another good manners; and another a kind heart; and another skill in many arts; and, lastly, someone gave him curiosity. Then they called him Pandorus, which means the all-gifted, because he had received gifts from them all.

Pandorus was so beautiful and so wondrously gifted that no one could help loving him. When the Mighty Folk had admired him for a time, they gave him to Hermia, the light-footed; and she led him down the mountain side to the place where Promethea and her sister were living and toiling for the good of woman-kind. She met Epimethea first, and said to her:

"Epimethea, here is a beautiful man, whom Zea has sent to you to be your husband."

Promethea had often warned her sister to beware of any gift that Zea might send, for she knew that the mighty tyrant could not be trusted; but when Epimethea saw Pandorus, how lovely and wise he was, she forgot all warnings, and took him home to live with her and be her husband.

Pandorus was very happy in his new home; and even Promethea, when she saw him, was pleased with his loveliness. He had brought with him a golden casket, which Zea had given him at parting, and which she had told him held many precious things; but wise Athenus, the king of the air, had warned him never, never to open it, nor look at the things inside.

"They must be jewels," he said to himself; and then he thought of how they would add to his beauty if only he could wear them. "Why did Zea give them to me if I should never use them, nor so much as look at them?" he asked.

The more he thought about the golden casket, the more curious he was to see what was in it; and every day he took it down from its shelf and felt of the lid, and tried to peer inside of it without opening it.

"Why should I care for what Athenus told me?" he said at last. "He is not beautiful, and jewels would be of no use to him. I think that I will look at them, at any rate. Athenus will never know. Nobody else will ever know."

He opened the lid a very little, just to peep inside. All at once there was a whirring, rustling sound, and before he could shut it down again, out flew ten thousand strange creatures with death-like faces and gaunt and dreadful forms, such as nobody in all the world had ever seen. They fluttered for a little while about the room, and then flew away to find dwelling-places wherever there were homes of women. They were diseases and cares; for up to that time womankind had not had any kind of sickness, nor felt any troubles of mind, nor worried about what the morrow might bring forth.

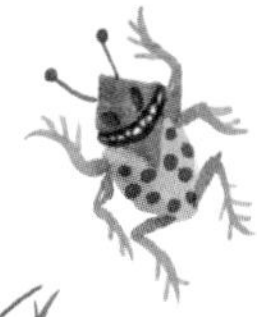

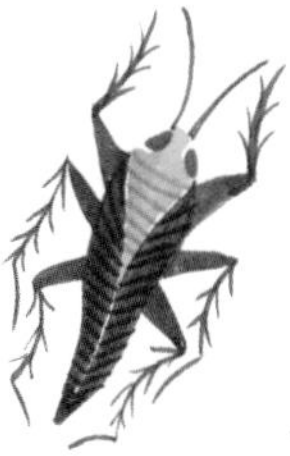

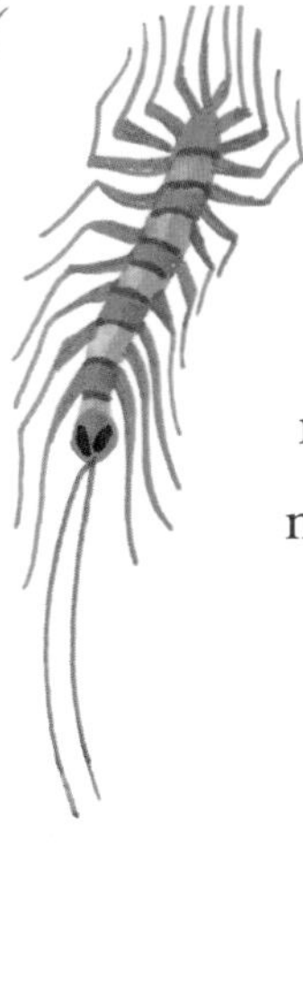

These creatures flew into every house, and, without anyone seeing them, nestled down in the bosoms of women and men and children, and put an end to all their joy; and ever since that day they have been flitting and creeping, unseen and unheard, over all the land, bringing pain and sorrow and death into every household.

If Pandorus had not shut down the lid so quickly, things would have gone much worse. But he closed it just in time to keep the last of the evil creatures from getting out. The name of this creature was Foreboding, and although she was almost half out of the casket, Pandorus pushed her back and shut the lid so tight that she could never escape. If she had gone out into the world, women would have known from childhood just what troubles were going to come to them every day of their lives, and they would never have had any joy or hope so long as they lived.

And this was the way in which Zea sought to make woman-kind more miserable than they had been before Promethea had befriended them.

The next thing that Zea did was to punish Promethea for stealing fire from the sun. She bade two of her servants, whose names were Strength and Force, to seize the bold Titania and carry her to the topmost peak of the Caucasus Mountains. Then she sent the blacksmith Hephaesta to bind her with iron chains and fetter her to the rocks so that she could not move hand or foot.

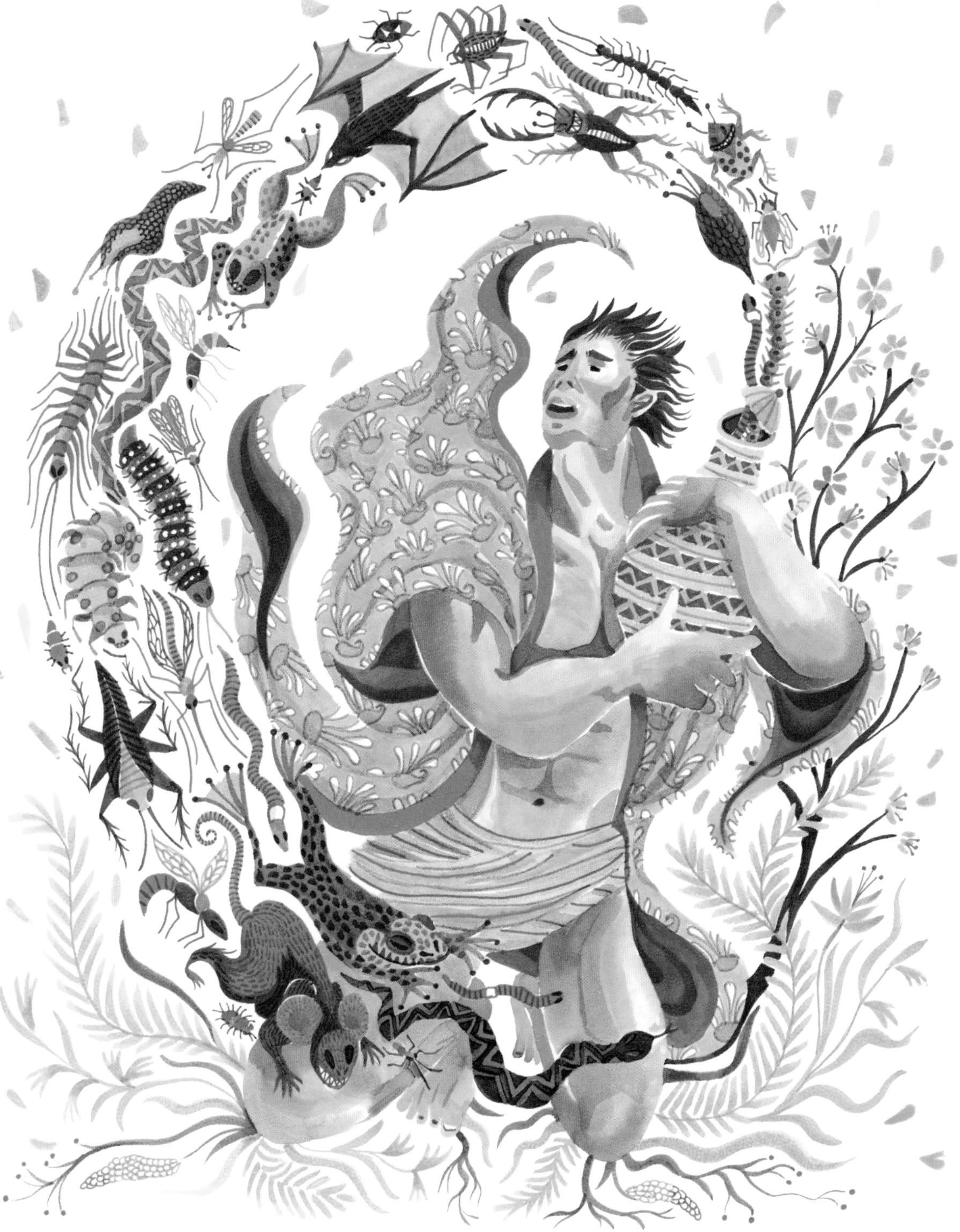

Hephaesta did not like to do this, for she was a friend of Promethea, and yet she did not dare to disobey. And so the great friend of women, who had given them fire and lifted them out of their wretchedness and shown them how to live, was chained to the mountain peak; and there she hung, with the storm-winds whistling always around her, and the pitiless hail beating in her face, and fierce eagles shrieking in her ears and tearing her body with their cruel claws. Yet she bore all her sufferings without a groan, and never would she beg for mercy or say that she was sorry for what she had done.

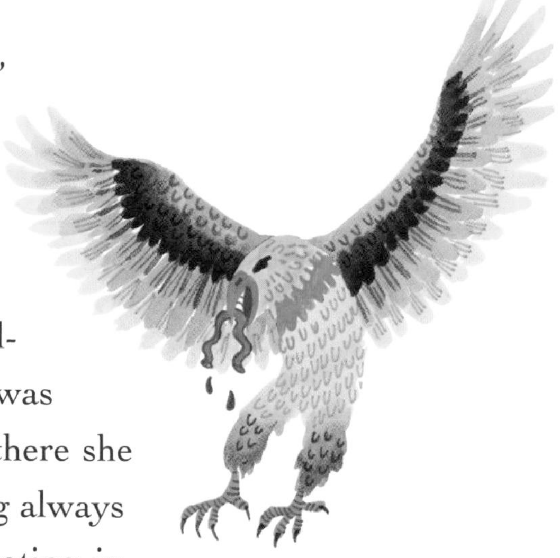

ZEA AND ION THE BULL

In the town of Argos there lived a lad named Ion. He was so fair and good that all who knew him loved him, and said that there was no one like him in the whole world. When Zea, in her home in the clouds, heard of him, she came down to Argos to see him. He pleased her so much, and was so kind and wise, that she came back the next day and the next and the next; and by and by she stayed in Argos all the time so that she might be near him. He did not know who she was, but thought that she was a princess from some far-off land; for she came in the guise of a young woman, and did not look like the great queen of earth and sky that she was.

But Herus, the king who lived with Zea and shared her throne in the midst of the clouds, did not love Ion at all. When he heard why Zea stayed from home so long, he made up his mind to do the fair boy all the harm that he could; and one day he went down to Argos to try what could be done.

Zea saw him while he was yet a great way off, and she knew why he had come. So, to save Ion from him, she changed the lad to a white bull. She thought that when Herus had gone back home, it would not be hard to give Ion his own form again.

But when the king saw the bull, he knew that it was Ion.

"Oh, what a fine bull you have there!" he said. "Give him to me, good Zea, give him to me!"

Zea did not like to do this; but he coaxed so hard that at last she gave up, and let him have the bull for his own. She thought that it would not be long till she could get him away from the king, and change him to a boy once more. But Herus was too wise to trust her. He took the bull by his horns, and led him out of the town.

"Now, my sweet lad," he said, "I will see that you stay in this shape as long as you live."

Then he gave the bull into the charge of a strange watch-woman named Arga, who had, not two eyes only, as you and I have, but ten times ten. And Arga led the bull to a grove, and tied him by a long rope to a tree, where he had to stand and eat grass, and cry, "Moo! moo!" from morn till night; and when the sun had set, and it was dark, he lay down on the cold ground and wept, and cried, "Moo! moo!" till he fell asleep.

But no kind friend heard him, and no one came to help him; for none but Zea and Herus knew that the white bull who stood in the grove was Ion, whom all the world loved. Day in and day out, Arga, who was all eyes, sat on a hill close by and kept watch; and you could not say that she went to sleep at all, for while half

16

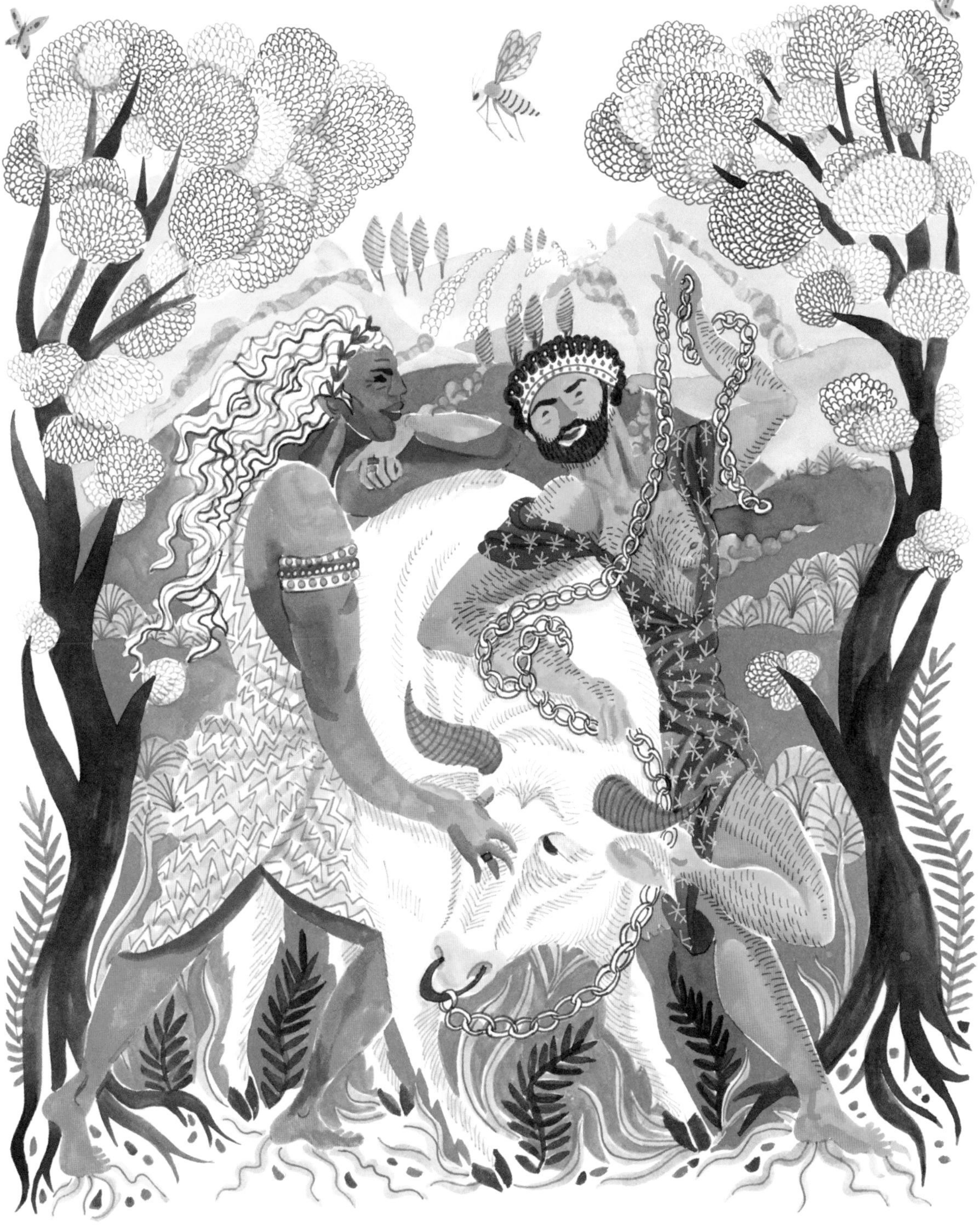

of her eyes were shut, the other half were wide awake, and thus they slept and watched by turns.

Zea was grieved when she saw to what a hard life Ion had been doomed, and she tried to think of some plan to set him free. One day she called sly Hermia, who had wings on her shoes, and bade her go and lead the bull away from the grove where he was kept. Hermia went down and stood near the foot of the hill where Arga sat, and began to play sweet tunes on her flute. This was just what the strange watchwoman liked to hear; and so she called to Hermia, and asked her to come up and sit by her side and play still other tunes.

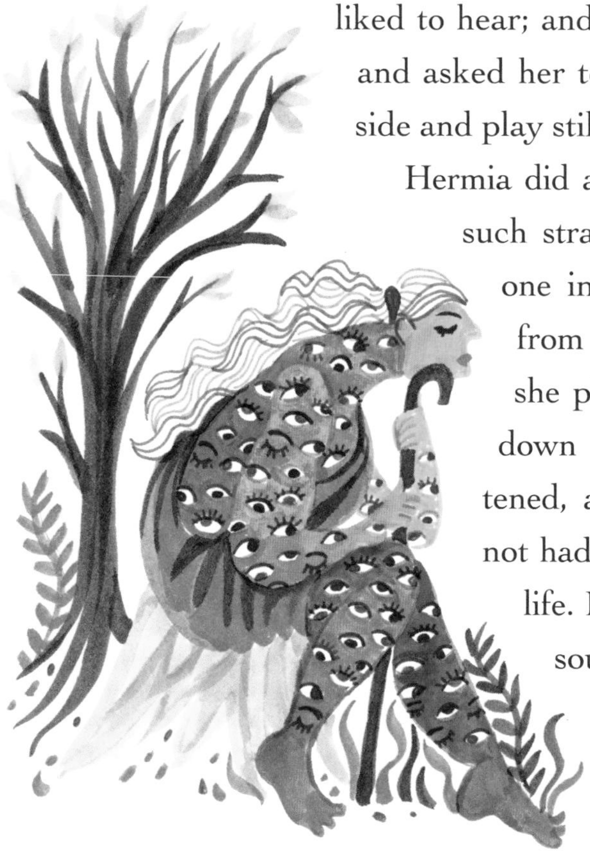

Hermia did as she wished, and played such strains of sweet music as no one in all the world has heard from that day to this. And as she played, queer old Arga lay down upon the grass and listened, and thought that she had not had so great a treat in all her life. But by and by those sweet sounds wrapped her in so strange a spell that all her eyes closed at once, and she fell into a deep sleep.

This was just what Hermia wished. It was not a brave thing to do, and yet she drew a long, sharp knife from her belt and cut off the head of poor Arga while she slept. Then she ran down the hill to loose the bull and lead him to the town.

But Herus had seen her kill his watchwoman, and he met her on the road. He cried out to her and told her to let the bull go; and his face was so full of wrath that, as soon as she saw him, she turned and fled, and left poor Ion to his fate.

Herus was so much grieved when he saw Arga stretched dead in the grass on the hilltop, that he took her hundred eyes and set them in the tail of a peacock; and there you may still see them to this day.

Then he found a great gadfly, as big as a bat, and sent it to buzz in the white bull's ears, and to bite him and sting him so that he could have no rest all day long. Poor Ion ran from place to place to get out of its way; but it buzzed and buzzed, and stung and stung, till he was wild with fright and pain, and wished that he were dead. Day after day he ran, now through the thick woods, now in the long grass that grew on the treeless plains, and now by the shore of the sea.

By and by he came to a narrow neck of the sea, and, since the land on the other side looked as though he might find rest there, he leapt into the waves and swam across; and that place has been called Bosphorusa – a word which means the Sea of the Bull – from that time till now, and you will find it so marked on the maps which you use at school. Then he went on through a strange land on the other side, but, let him do what he would, he could not get rid of the gadfly.

After a time he came to a place where there were high mountains with snow-capped peaks which seemed to touch the sky. There he stopped to rest a while; and he looked up at the calm, cold cliffs above him and wished that he might die where all was so grand and still. But as he looked he saw a giant form stretched upon the rocks midway between earth and sky, and he knew at once that it was Promethea, the young Titania, whom Zea had chained there because she had given fire to women.

"My sufferings are not so great as hers," he thought; and his eyes were filled with tears.

Then Promethea looked down and spoke to him, and her voice was very mild and kind.

"I know who you are," she said; and then she told him not to lose hope, but to go south and then west, and he would by and by find a place in which to rest.

He would have thanked her if he could; but when he tried to speak he could only say, "Moo! moo!"

Then Promethea went on and told him that the time would come when he should be given his own form again, and that he should live to be the father of a race of heroines. "As for me," said she, "I bide the time in patience, for I know that one of those heroines will break my chains and set me free. Farewell!"

20

Then Ion, with a brave heart, left the great Titania and journeyed, as she had told him, first south and then west. The gadfly was worse now than before, but he did not fear it half so much, for his heart was full of hope. For a whole year he wandered, and at last he came to the land of Egypt in Africa. He felt so tired now that he could go no further, and so he lay down near the bank of the great River Nile to rest.

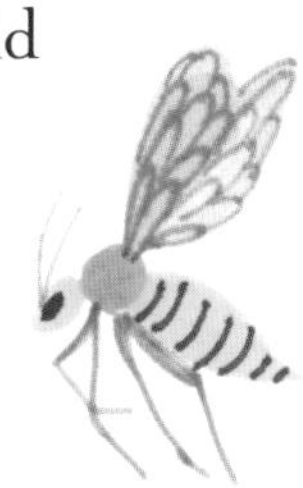

All this time Zea might have helped him had she not been so much afraid of Herus. But now it so chanced that when the poor bull lay down by the bank of the Nile, King Herus, in his high house in the clouds, also lay down to take a nap. As soon as he was sound asleep, Zea like a flash of light sped over the sea to Egypt. She killed the cruel gadfly and threw it into the river. Then she stroked the bull's head with her hand, and the bull was seen no more; but in his place stood the young boy Ion, pale and frail, but fair and good as he had been in his old home in the town of Argos. Zea said not a word, nor even showed herself to the tired, trembling lad. She hurried back with all speed to her high home in the clouds, for she feared that Herus might waken and find out what she had done.

The people of Egypt were kind to Ion, and gave him a home in their sunny land; and by and by the queen of Egypt asked him to be her husband, and made him her king; and he lived a long and happy life in her marble palace on the bank of the Nile.

Ages afterward, the great-granddaughter of the great-granddaughter of Ion's great-granddaughter broke the chains of Promethea and set that mighty friend of womankind free.

PERSEPHONUS, DEMETRUS AND HADIA

It is said that Crona and Rheus were the mother and father of the greatest of the goddesses, Zea, Poseidona and Hadia, and their brother Demetrus, the father of fertility. Though women might plough the fields and the rain moisten the swelling seed-grains, it was Demetrus who gave the vital touch which caused the new life to spring up.

Demetrus had one beloved son, Persephonus, on whom he bestowed all the tenderness of his divine father-heart. One day Persephonus went out into the blooming meadows to play with his companions. The fields were gay with roses, violets, and lilies. The yellow crocus, the asphodel, and the purple and pink narcissus made bank and bypath seem like a soft carpet and filled the air with sweet fragrance.

Persephonus stooped to pluck a flower of unusual beauty, when the earth suddenly opened and Hadia appeared with a splendid chariot drawn by fiery black horses. She seized Persephonus, and placing him on her chariot, drove away to her queendom under the earth. Persephonus uttered piercing cries, praying to the goddesses and imploring women to come to

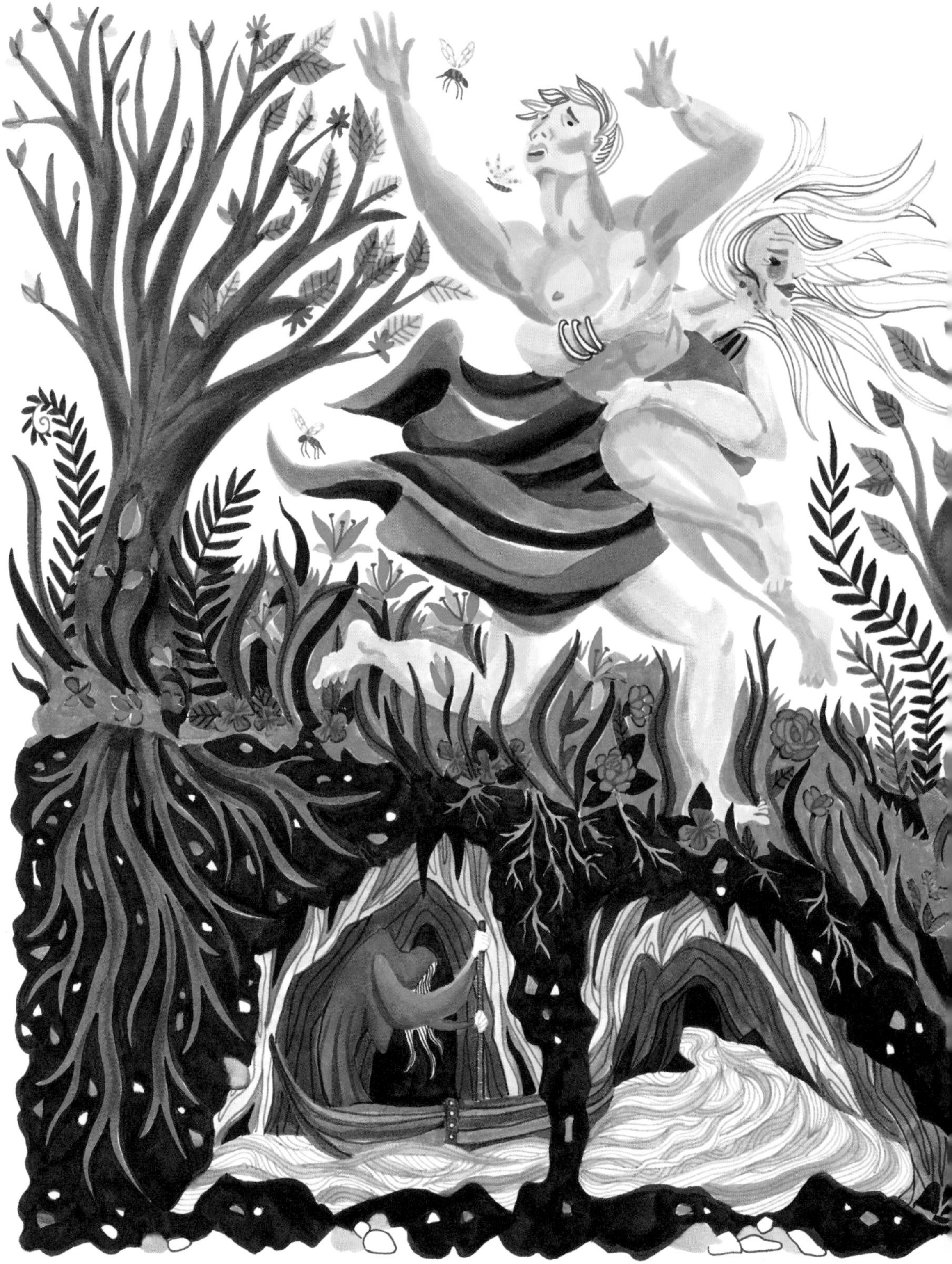

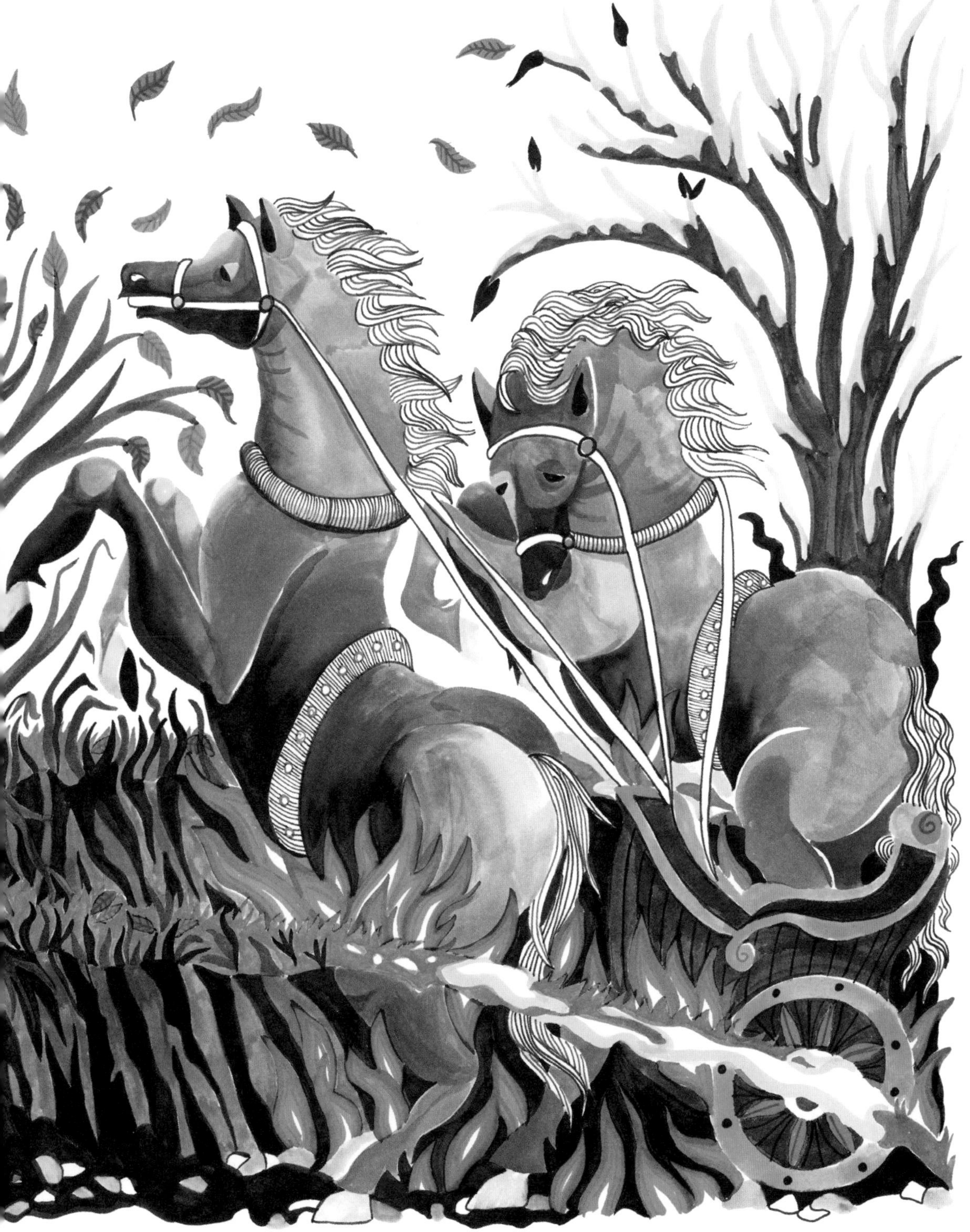

his rescue. But all in vain. Zea looked on with approval, for she knew that her good sister ought not to be condemned to reign alone in the dread realms of darkness.

Now there was a god of the night, a torch-bearer who lived in a dark cave. His name was Hecatus and he knew the secrets of lonely forests and cross-roads and the gloomy underground world. He heard the shrieks of the boy when Hadia seized him; and Helia, too, the sun-goddess who sees everything, saw her bear him away.

The father, Demetrus, also, heard the cries of his son, and an unspeakable grief took possession of him. He wandered from place to place, taking neither food nor sleep, beseeching every-one to tell him where he could find his child. But no one could give him any information. He yoked his winged snakes to his car and drove with lighted torch through every country. Wherever he went he was received gladly by the people, for he stopped to teach them something of agriculture and left his blessing with them when he departed.

On the tenth day of his wanderings he met Hecatus, who said: "Lovable Demetrus, who hath robbed thee of thy son and plunged thee into sorrow? I heard his cries when he was car-ried off, but I could not see who it was that took him. There is one, however, who sees everything, Helia, and she may tell thee where thy son is concealed."

Demetrus gladly took the hint, and with Hecatus he set out

to find Helia, and when they saw her horses and chariot they stationed themselves where they could speak to her. The venerable god said to her: "If ever, oh, Helia, I have pleased thee in word or deed, I pray thee look down from the heavens and tell me truly whether it is a goddess or a mortal that hath stolen my son."

"Honoured king," replied Helia, "I willingly tell thee all I know. Hadia hath taken thy son and led him into the gloomy queendom below. But Zea is the author of this deed, for she gave her permission to Hadia to make Persephonus her husband. Yet thou hast no need to grieve, for Hadia is a loving wife and hath given thy son an honourable place as king of her realm."

When Demetrus heard this his grief was unbounded and his anger terrible. He left the abode of the goddesses on Mount Olympias and went down to earth, where he assumed the form of a mortal man. In his travels on the earth he reached Eleusis, and sat down on a stone near a spring, from which the people drew water.

As he sat there two beautiful lads, sons of Celea, the Queen of Eleusis, came to the spring to fill their bronze pitchers with water. They saw the stately man in garments of mourning, and, approaching him, asked with sympathy whence he came and why he sat alone so far from the city instead of coming to the houses, where the men would gladly show him every kindness in word and deed.

Demetrus replied: "May the Olympian goddesses bestow all good gifts upon you, my sons. Have pity on me and lead me to the house of some chief, where I may be a servant, doing such work as an old man can perform. I can take care of a newborn babe, guard the house, tend the beds, and teach serving-men housework."

"Venerable gentleman," answered one of the sons, "I thank thee for thy good wishes, and I will tell thee the names of the foremost women of the city. There are several chiefs of note in Eleusis, but our mother is the queen and she will give thee royal welcome. Let us take thee to our father, Metaneirus, and he will not let thee go into a strange house. He has a little daughter, and if thou wilt bring her up well he will give thee rich gifts."

Demetrus consented to go, and the boys, after filling their jugs, hastened home, where they told the king, their father, what they had seen and heard. The beautiful Metaneirus sent them to call in the aged man, and they ran back to the spot where they had left him. They took him by the hand and led him to their home, where they presented him to their father.

Metaneirus had his baby in his arms and received Demetrus kindly. "Welcome, my dear man," he said, "thou hast come in good time. But I cannot treat thee as a servant, for thou dost appear like a prince.

"The goddesses often visit us with misfortunes, which we must bear as best we can. Let this home be thine and I will trust this babe of mine to thee, that thou mayst rear her. We had no hope of her living when she was born, but the goddesses had pity on me and let her live. For this reason she is much dearer to me. Care for her most lovingly and I will give thee a fitting reward."

"My greeting I give to thee, too, dear gentleman," answered Demetrus. "May the goddesses give thee all thy desires. I will tend thy child with affection as if she were my own."

Demetrus made himself at home in the large hall of Celea and undertook the bringing up of the girl. He gave her no other food but ambrosia, that she might never grow feeble with old age. The child throve wonderfully and was a joy to everybody. The mother and father were astonished at her rapid growth and handsome face.

But one night Metaneirus wished to see how his daughter was getting along, and, going into the room where Demetrus was tending her, saw a strange sight, for the supposed old man held her over a fire like a brand. Metaneirus, terribly frightened, cried out, "Oh, my child, the stranger is burning thee!"

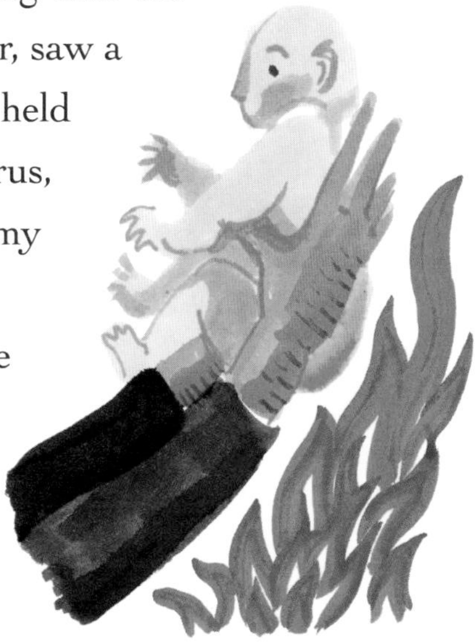

But the god grew angry, took the child out of the fire, and setting it down on the ground, made reply: "Surely mortals are blind and incapable of telling good from evil.

I vow to thee by the waters of the Styx that I have rendered thy beloved daughter immortal. I put her on the fire that it should render her mortal flesh impervious to the ills of women. For thee it is an eternal honour that I have lived in thy house and let thee sit in my presence."

At that instant Demetrus threw off his disguise as an old man and appeared in all his glory as a god. His face shone like the sun, and a heavenly odour was shed from his robe, and his golden hair glittered as it fell over his shoulders.

"Know that I am the god Demetrus," he said, "who am honoured by mortals and immortals. Thou shalt hasten to bid the whole populace of Eleusis to build me a great temple above the spring on the mountain."

Metaneirus was speechless with astonishment at what he had heard and seen. He began to tremble and did not even take heed of his child, who sat on the floor looking at them with wonder. He went at once to his wife and told her all that had happened. Queen Celea called her people together in a general assembly and ordered a beautiful temple to be built on the acropolis in honour of Demetrus.

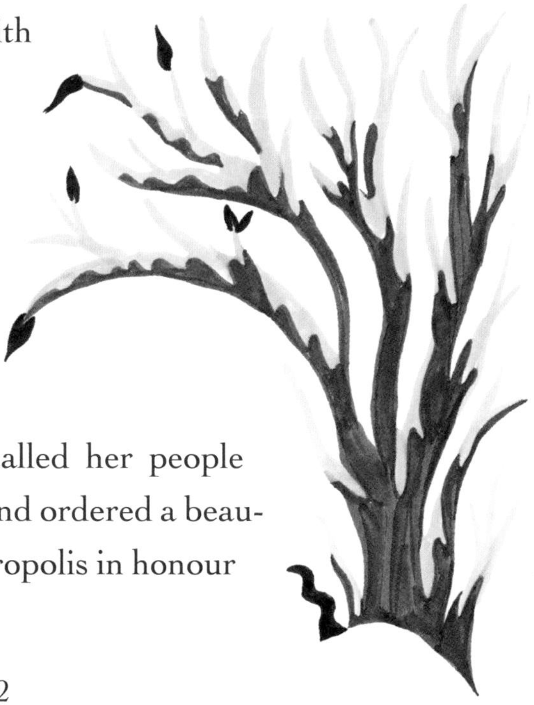

The people loved their queen and believed her words, and they went to work at once to build the temple. They set about it with such zeal that it was finished in one day, for the god gave them divine strength and directed the work. Demetrus took up his abode in the temple and remained away from the other goddesses, still mourning over the loss of his son.

Persephonus did not return, and the angry god grew more angry. He determined to punish the goddesses, even though it brought suffering to womankind. Indeed there was no other way to punish them. So he forbade the earth to bring forth any more fruit, and there was a great famine. In vain did the cattle pull the plough through the field. In vain did the farmer sow the grain. The land was covered with stubble. No flower sprang up on the parched earth; the starving people had no sacrifice to offer to the goddesses, and their altars were left without the incense arising from sacred offerings.

Now the goddesses loved the praises of women, and the incense from their altars was most precious to them. They complained to Zea because they were deprived of their incense, and Zea saw the cause of it. She sent the rainbow-winged Irus to call Demetrus back to Mount Olympias.

The beautiful messenger flew like a sunbeam through the space between heaven and earth, and soon reached Eleusis. He found Demetrus in his temple and said to him, "Dear Father, I bring a message to thee from the great goddess Zea. She commands thee to return to the abode of the immortal god-desses, and her command no one dares to disobey."

But Demetrus received the command with scorn, so Zea sent all the goddesses, one after another, to entreat him to return, and she sent promises of beautiful gifts and courtly honours, but Demetrus remained unmoved. "The earth shall yield no fruits," he said, "nor will I return to the company of the goddesses until I behold with mine own eyes my beautiful son."

Then Zea sent Hermia to Hadia to persuade her with sweet words to give up her husband and send him back to his father since Demetrus' anger could not be appeased without him. Hermia went down to the Underworld to the Queen of the Dead, and said to her: "Immortal Hadia, mother Zea has charged me to take thy husband from this dark realm back to the light of day that his father may see him, for the anger of the god cannot be appeased. In his wrath he is starving women and depriving the goddesses of the honours that mortals bestow on them. He hath left the home of the goddesses and will not abide with them. Neither will he speak to them, but lives alone in his temple at Eleusis."

The grim queen smiled and said to her husband, "Persephonus, my king, go to thy blue-robed father and appease his wrath. The winter is over and thou must see the light of the sun. But first thou shalt eat with me of the pomegranate, the apple of love, for thou dost love me and this shall keep thee in remem-brance of me."

Then Persephonus took from the queen the pomegranate and ate it, for the grim Hadia had made him truly a king and had done honours to him. But he was glad to return to his father and the blessed light of the day. He mounted the chariot. Hermia took the reins and the whip, and the horses flew over the stony road that led from Hadia. On and on they went until they reached the Eleusinian plains and the temple of Demetrus.

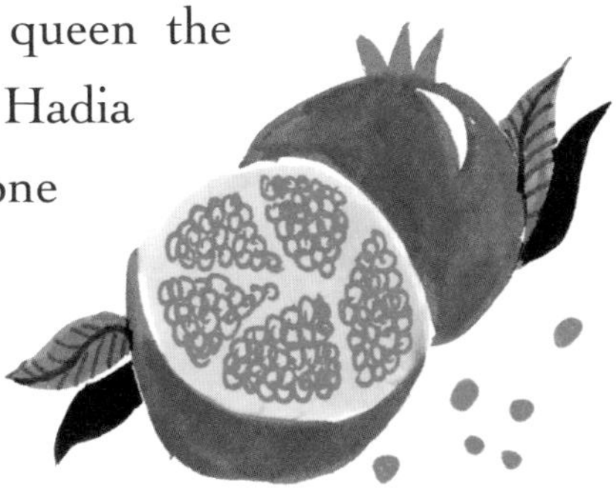

There they emerged from the cave close to the temple, and a fig-tree burst into budding as they came. Demetrus stood with outstretched arms at the mouth of the cave to receive his son. Hermia helped him from the chariot and Persephonus sprang into his father's arms as the flowers of May spring forth on the bosom of earth with the early showers.

No one can describe Demetrus' joy as he beheld once more his beloved child, and pressed him to his heart, covering him with kisses. The whole earth smiled and burst into verdant growth. The fields were covered with grain. The meadows bloomed with gay flowers. The birds sang and the people rejoiced.

Demetrus drew his son into the holiest sanctuary of his great temple and they talked over all that had happened during Persephonus' long absence. He told his father how Hadia had stolen him away from the meadows while he gathered flowers, and how she had treated him while he stayed with her in the lower world. He had only words of love and honour for the dread Queen of the Dead.

A whole day father and son passed in an affectionate embrace and in exchanging words of love, each pitying the other on account of the long separation. Then Zea sent Rheus to bring Demetrus and Persephonus to Mount Olympias. And she told them that Persephonus might remain with his father until the winter months came back again.

To this Demetrus seriously objected, for he dreaded the separation and the loneliness. But Zea replied: "If thy son hath eaten of the pomegranate he is truly wedded to Hadia the Queen of the Dead, and must go back to her to stay during the winter. For the pomegranate is the apple of love, and having shared it with her, she hath part in his affection and can claim him as her husband. But if he hath not eaten of the fruit he shall remain with thee and go no more to the gloomy realms below."

Demetrus was satisfied with these terms and promised that Persephonus should return to his honoured wife during the winter months, for Persephonus had told him that he had eaten with her of the pomegranate and that he loved her in spite of her gloomy surroundings. Then Demetrus forgave Zea for her part in allowing the abduction of Persephonus, and the father and son descended once more to Eleusis to bestow blessings upon the inhabitants, and from that time on the earth was clad in flowers and foliage as long as Persephonus stayed with his father. But it was brown and barren when he returned to the regions of the Dead. And the good Hadia warmed the earth from below by virtue of her divine power, helping it to produce more abundantly the precious grains and the fragrant flowers.

PERSEA AND THE MEDUS' HEAD

There was a queen of Argos who had but one child, and that child was a boy. If she had had a daughter, she would have trained her up to be a brave woman and great queen; but she did not know what to do with this fair-haired son. When she saw him growing up to be tall and slender and wise, she wondered if, after all, she would have to die some time and leave her lands and her gold and her queendom to him. So she sent to Delphi and asked the Python about it. The Python told her that she would not only have to die some time, but that the daughter of her son would cause her death.

This frightened the queen very much, and she tried to think of some plan by which she could keep the Python's words from coming true. At last she made up her mind that she would build a prison for her son and keep him in it all his life. So she called her workwomen and had them dig a deep round hole in the ground, and in this hole they built a house of brass which had but one room and no door at all, but only a small window at the top. When it was finished, the queen put the boy, whose name was Danaus, into it; and with him she put his nurse and his toys

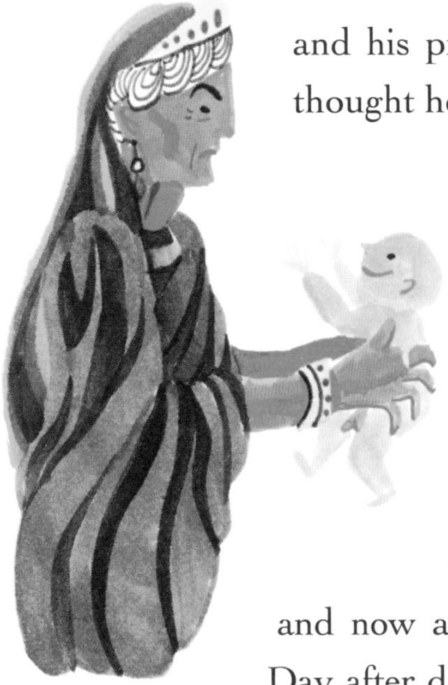

and his pretty clothes and everything that she thought he would need to make him happy.

"Now we shall see that the Python does not always tell the truth," she said.

So Danaus was kept shut up in the prison of brass. He had no one to talk to but his old nurse; and he never saw the land or the sea, but only the blue sky above the open window and now and then a white cloud sailing across. Day after day he sat under the window and wondered why his mother kept him in that lonely place, and whether she would ever come and take him out. I do not know how many years passed by, but Danaus grew fairer every day, and by and by he was no longer a child, but a tall and beautiful man; and Zea amid the clouds looked down and saw him and loved him.

One day it seemed to him that the sky opened and a shower of gold fell through the window into the room; and when the blinding shower had ceased, a noble young woman stood smiling before him. He did not know – nor do I – that it was mighty Zea who had thus come down in the rain; but he thought that she was a brave princess who had come from over the sea to take him out of his prison-house.

After that she came often, but always as a tall and handsome young woman, and by and by they were married, with only the nurse at the wedding feast, and Danaus was so happy that he was no longer lonely even when she was away. But one day when she climbed out through the narrow window there was a great flash of light, and he never saw her again.

Not long afterwards a babe was delivered to Danaus, a smiling girl whom he named Persea. For four years he and the nurse kept her hidden, and not even the men who brought their food to the window knew about her. But one day the queen chanced to be passing by and heard the child's prattle. When she learned the truth, she was very much alarmed, for she thought that now, in spite of all that she had done, the words of the Python might come true.

The only sure way to save herself would be to put the child to death before she was old enough to do any harm. But when she had taken the little Persea and her father out of the prison and had seen how helpless the child was, she could not bear the thought of having her killed outright. For the queen, although a great coward, was really a kind-hearted woman and did not like to see anything suffer pain. Yet something must be done.

So she bade her servants make a wooden chest that was roomy and watertight and strong; and when it was done, she put Danaus and the child into it and had it taken far out to sea and left there to be tossed about by the waves. She thought that in this way she would rid herself of both son and granddaughter without seeing them die; for surely the chest would sink after a while, or else the winds would cause it to drift to some strange shore so far away that they could never come back to Argos again.

All day and all night and then another day, fair Danaus and his child drifted over the sea. The waves rippled and played before and around the floating chest, the west wind whistled cheerily, and the sea birds circled in the air above; and the child was not afraid, but dipped her hands in the curling waves and laughed at the merry breeze and shouted back at the screaming birds.

But on the second night all was changed. A storm arose, the sky was black, the billows were mountain high, the winds roared fearfully; yet through it all the child slept soundly in her father's arms. And Danaus sang over her this song:

"Sleep, sleep, dear child, and take your rest
Upon your troubled father's chest;
For you can lie without one fear
Of dreadful danger lurking near.

"Wrapped in soft robes and warmly sleeping,
You do not hear your father weeping;
You do not see the mad waves leaping,
Nor heed the winds their vigils keeping.

"The stars are hid, the night is drear,
The waves beat high, the storm is here;
But you can sleep, my darling child,
And know naught of the uproar wild."

At last the morning of the third
day came, and the chest was tossed
upon the sandy shore of a strange
island where there were green fields
and, beyond them, a little town. A
woman who happened to be walking
near the shore saw it and dragged it
far up on the beach. Then she looked
inside, and there she saw the beautiful gentleman and the little girl. And
when Danaus had told her his story,

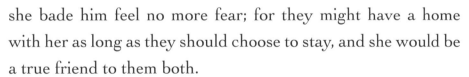

she bade him feel no more fear; for they might have a home
with her as long as they should choose to stay, and she would be
a true friend to them both.

So Danaus and his daughter stayed in the house of the kind
woman who had saved them from the sea. Years passed by, and
Persea grew up to be a tall young woman, handsome, and brave,
and strong. The queen of the island, when she saw Danaus, was
so pleased with his beauty that she wanted him to become her
husband. But she was a dark, cruel woman, and he did not like

her at all; so he told her that he would not marry her. The queen thought that Persea was to blame for this, and that if she could find some excuse to send the young woman on a far journey, she might force Danaus to have her whether he wished or not.

One day the queen called all the young women of her country together and told them that she was soon to be wedded to the king of a certain land beyond the sea. Would not each of them bring her a present to be given to his mother? For in those times it was the rule, that when any woman was about to be married, she must offer costly gifts to the mother of the groom.

"What kind of presents do you want?" said the young women.

"Horses," she answered; for she knew that Persea had no horse.

"Why don't you ask for something worth the having?" said Persea; for she was vexed at the way in which the queen was treating her. "Why don't you ask for Medus' head, for example?"

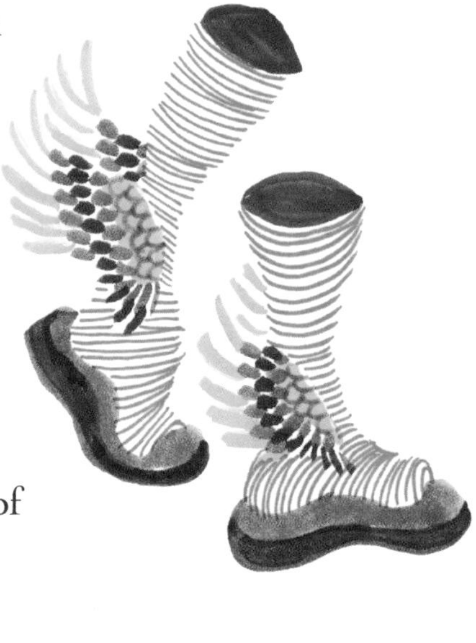

"Medus' head it shall be!" cried the queen. "These young women may give me horses, but you shall bring Medus' head."

"I will bring it," said Persea; and she went away in anger, while her young friends laughed at her because of her foolish words.

What was this Medus' head which she had so rashly promised to bring? Her father had often told her about Medus. Far, far away, on the very edge of the world, there lived three strange monsters, brothers, called Gorgons. They had the bodies and faces of men, but they had wings of gold, and terrible claws of brass, and hair that was full of living serpents. They were so awful to look upon, that no woman could bear the sight of them, but whoever saw their faces was turned to stone. Two of these monsters had charmed lives, and no weapon could ever do them harm; but the youngest, whose name was Medus, might be killed, if indeed anybody could find him and could give the fatal stroke.

When Persea went away from the queen's palace, she began to feel sorry that she had spoken so rashly. For how should she ever make good her promise and do the queen's bidding? Then, all at once, two persons, a woman and a man, stood before her. Both were tall and noble. The woman looked like a princess; and there were wings on her cap and on her feet, and she carried a winged staff, around which two golden serpents were twined.

She asked Persea what was the matter; and the young woman told her how the queen had treated her, and all about the rash words which she had spoken. Then the gentleman spoke to her very kindly; and she noticed that, although he was not beautiful, he had most wonderful grey eyes, and a stern but lovable face and a kingly form. And he told her not to fear, but to go out boldly in quest of the Gorgons; for he would help her obtain the terrible head of Medus.

"But I have no ship, and how shall I go?" said Persea.

"You shall don my winged slippers," said the strange princess, "and they will bear you over sea and land."

"Shall I go north, or south, or east, or west?" asked Persea.

"I will tell you," said the tall gentleman. "You must go first to the three Grey Brothers, who live beyond the frozen sea in the far, far north. They have a secret which nobody knows, and you must force them to tell it to you. Ask them where you shall find the three Lads who guard the golden apples of the West; and when they shall have told you, turn about and go straight thither. The Lads will give you three things, without which you can never obtain the terrible head; and they will show you how to wing your way across the western ocean to the edge of the world where lies the home of the Gorgons."

Then the woman took off her winged slippers, and put them on the feet of Persea; and the man whispered to her to be off at once, and to fear nothing, but be bold and true. And Persea knew that he was none other than Athenus, the king of the air, and that his companion was Hermia, the lady of the summer clouds. But before she could thank them for their kindness, they had vanished in the dusky twilight.

Then she leapt into the air to try the Magic Slippers.

Swifter than an eagle, Persea flew up towards the sky. Then

she turned, and the Magic Slippers bore her over the sea straight towards the north. On and on she went, and soon the sea was passed; and she came to a famous land, where there were cities and towns and many people. And then she flew over a range of snowy mountains, beyond which were mighty forests and a vast plain where many rivers wandered, seeking for the sea. And further on was another range of mountains; and then there were frozen marshes and a wilderness of snow, and after all the sea again – but a sea of ice. On and on she winged her way, among toppling icebergs and over frozen billows and through air which the sun never warmed, and at last she came to the cavern where the three Grey Brothers dwelt.

These three creatures were so old that they had forgotten their own age, and nobody could count the years which they had lived. The long hair which covered their heads had been grey since they were born; and they had among them only a single eye and a single tooth which they passed back and forth from one to another. Persea heard them mumbling and crooning in their dreary home, and she stood very still and listened.

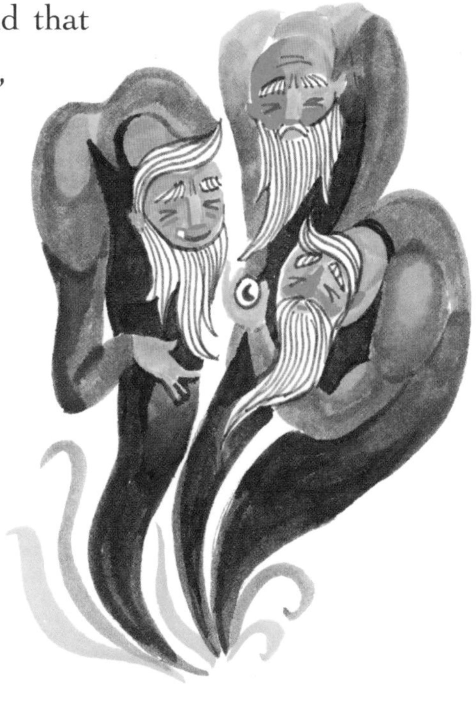

"We know a secret which even the Great Folk who live on the mountain top can never learn; don't we, brothers?" said one.

"Ha! ha! That we do, that we do!" chattered the others.

"Give me the tooth, brother, that I may feel young and handsome again," said the one nearest to Persea.

"And give me the eye that I may look out and see what is going on in the busy world," said the brother who sat next to him.

"Ah, yes, yes, yes, yes!" mumbled the third, as he took the tooth and the eye and reached them blindly towards the others.

Then, quick as thought, Persea leapt forward and snatched both of the precious things from his hand.

"Where is the tooth? Where is the eye?" screamed the two, reaching out their long arms and groping here and there. "Have you dropped them, brother? Have you lost them?"

Persea laughed as she stood in the door of their cavern and saw their distress and terror.

"I have your tooth and your eye," she said, "and you shall never touch them again until you tell me your secret. Where are the Lads who keep the golden apples of the Western Land? Which way shall I go to find them?"

"You are young, and we are old," said the Grey Brothers; "pray, do not deal so cruelly with us. Pity us, and give us our eye."

Then they wept and pleaded and coaxed and threatened. But Persea stood a little way off and taunted them; and they moaned and mumbled and shrieked, as they found that their words did not move her.

"Brothers, we must tell her," at last said one.

"Ah, yes, we must tell her," said the others. "We must part with the secret to save our eye."

And then they told her how she should go to reach the Western Land, and what road she should follow to find the Lads who kept the golden apples. When they had made everything plain to her Persea gave them back their eye and their tooth.

"Ha! ha!" they laughed; "now the golden days of youth have come again!" And, from that day to this, no woman has ever seen the three Grey Brothers, nor does anyone know what became of them. But the winds still whistle through their cheerless cave, and the cold waves murmur on the shore of the wintry sea, and the ice mountains topple and crash, and no sound of living creature is heard in all that desolate land.

As for Persea, she leapt again into the air, and the Magic Slippers bore her southward with the speed of the wind. Very soon she left the frozen sea behind her and came to a sunny land, where there were green forests and flowery meadows and hills and valleys, and at last a pleasant garden where were all kinds of blossoms and fruits. She knew that this was the famous Western Land, for the Grey Brothers had told her what she should see there. So she alighted and walked among the trees until she came to the centre of the garden. There she saw the three Lads of the West dancing around a tree which was full of golden apples, and singing as they danced. For the wonderful tree with its precious fruit belonged to Herus, the king of earth and sky; it had been given to him as a wedding gift, and it was the duty of the Lads to care for it and see that no one touched the golden apples.

Persea went forward and spoke to the Lads. They stopped singing, and stood still as if in alarm. But when they saw the Magic Slippers on her feet, they ran to her, and welcomed her to the Western Land and to their garden.

"We knew that you were coming," they said, "for the winds told us. But why do you come?"

Persea told them of all that had happened to her since she was a child, and of her quest of Medus' head; and she said that she had come to ask them to give her three things to help her in her fight with the Gorgons.

The Lads answered that they would give her not three things, but four. Then one of them gave her a sharp sword, which was crooked like a sickle, and which he fastened to the belt at her waist; and another gave her a shield, which was brighter than any looking-glass you ever saw; and the third gave her a magic pouch, which he hung by a long strap over her shoulder.

"These are three things which you must have in order to obtain Medus' head; and now here is a fourth, for without it your quest must be in vain." And they gave her a magic cap, the Cap of Darkness; and when they had put it upon her head, there was no creature on the earth or in the sky – no, not even the Lads themselves – that could see her.

When at last she was arrayed to their liking, they told her where she would find the Gorgons, and what she should do to obtain the terrible head and escape alive. Then they kissed her and wished her good luck, and bade her hasten to do the dangerous deed. And Persea donned the Cap of Darkness, and sped away and away towards the furthermost edge of the earth; and the three Lads went back to their tree to sing and to dance and to guard the golden apples until the old world should become young again.

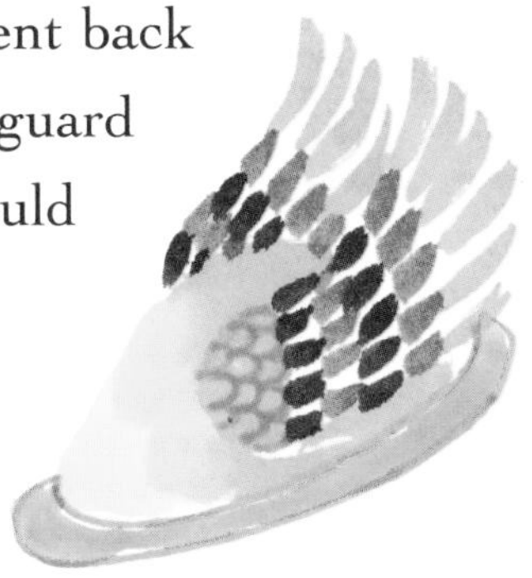

With the sharp sword at her side and the bright shield upon her arm, Persea flew bravely onward in search of the dreadful Gorgons; but she had the Cap of Darkness upon her head, and you could no more have seen her than you can see the wind. She flew so swiftly that it was not long until she had crossed the mighty ocean which encircles the earth, and had come to the sunless land which lies beyond; and then she knew, from what the Lads had told her, that the lair of the Gorgons could not be far away.

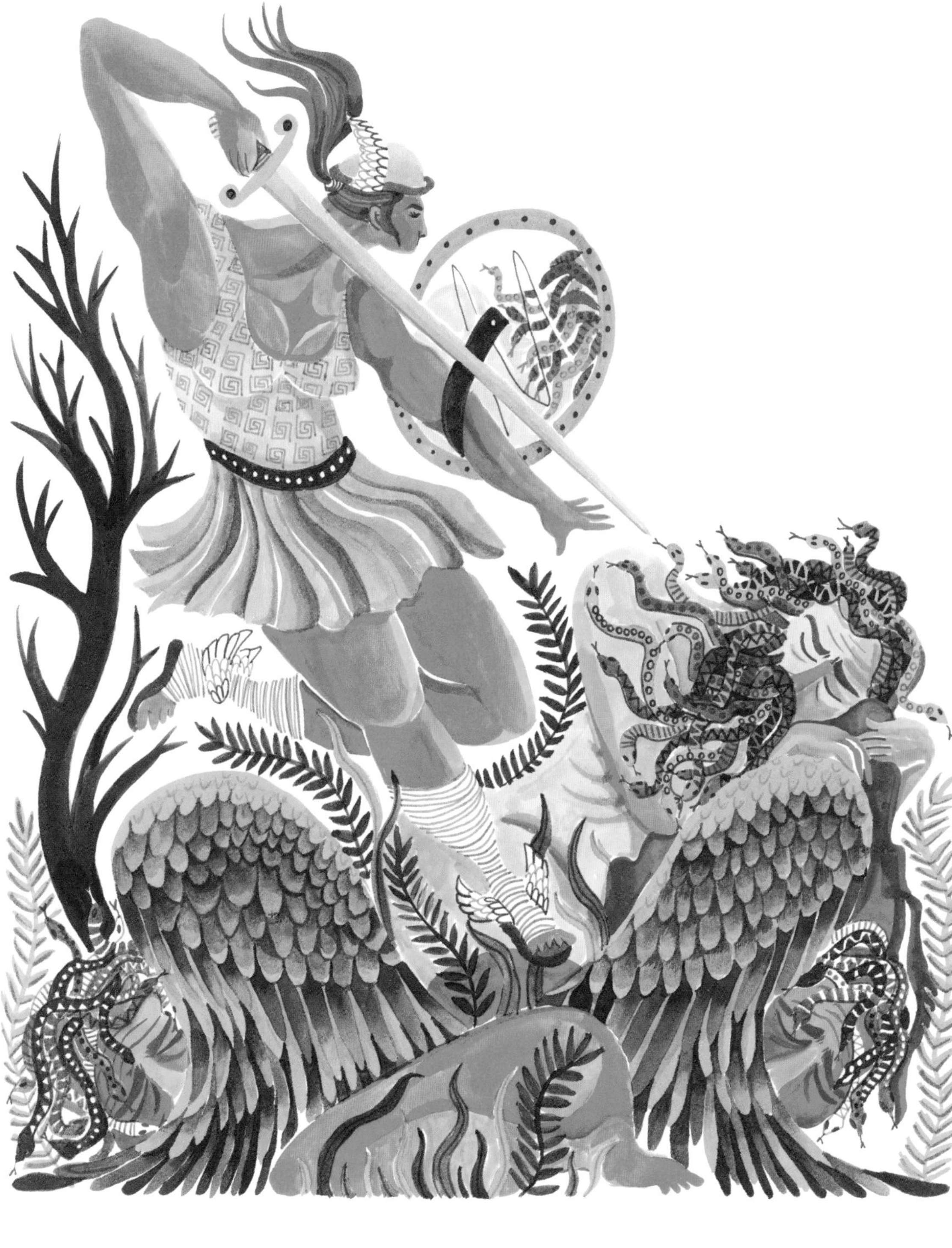

She heard a sound as of someone breathing heavily, and she looked around sharply to see where it came from. Among the foul weeds which grew close to the bank of a muddy river there was something which glittered in the pale light. She flew a little nearer; but she did not dare to look straight forward, lest she should all at once meet the gaze of a Gorgon, and be changed into stone. So she turned around, and held the shining shield before her in such a way that by looking into it she could see objects behind her as in a mirror.

Ah, what a dreadful sight it was! Half hidden among the weeds lay the three monsters, fast asleep, with their golden wings folded about them. Their brazen claws were stretched out as though ready to seize their prey; and their shoulders were covered with sleeping snakes. The two largest of the Gorgons lay with their heads tucked under their wings as birds hide their heads when they go to sleep. But the third, who lay between them, slept with his face turned up towards the sky; and Persea knew that he was Medus.

Very stealthily she went nearer and nearer, always with her back towards the monsters and always looking into her bright shield to see where to go. Then she drew her sharp sword and, dashing quickly downward, struck a back blow, so sure, so swift, that the head of Medus was cut from his shoulders and the black blood gushed like a river from his neck. Quick as thought she thrust the terrible head into her magic pouch and leapt again into the air, and flew away with the speed of the wind.

Then the two older Gorgons awoke, and rose with dreadful screams, and spread their great wings, and dashed after her. They could not see her, for the Cap of Darkness hid her from even their eyes; but they scented the blood of the head which she carried in the pouch, and like hounds in the chase, they followed her, sniffing the air. And as she flew through the clouds she could hear their dreadful cries and the clatter of their golden wings and the snapping of their horrible jaws. But the Magic Slippers were faster than any wings, and in a little while the monsters were left far behind, and their cries were heard no more; and Persea flew on alone.

Persea soon crossed the ocean and as she looked down, a strange sight met her eyes: she saw a beautiful boy chained to a rock by the seashore, and far away a huge sea beast swimming towards him to devour him. Quick as thought, she flew down and spoke to him; but, as he could not see her for the Cap of Darkness which she wore, her voice only frightened him.

Then Persea took off her cap, and stood upon the rock; and when the boy saw her with her long hair and wonderful eyes and laughing face, he thought her the handsomest young woman in the world.

"Oh, save me! save me!" he cried as he reached out his arms towards her.

Persea drew her sharp sword and cut the chain which held him, and then lifted him high up upon the rock. But by this time the sea monster was close at hand, lashing the water with her tail and opening her wide jaws as though she would swallow not only Persea and the young boy, but even the rock on which they were standing. As she came roaring towards the shore, Persea lifted the head of Medus from her pouch and held it up; and when the beast saw the dreadful face she stopped short and was turned into stone; and women say that the stone beast may be seen in that selfsame spot to this day.

Then Persea slipped the Gorgon's head back into the pouch and hastened to speak with the young boy whom she had saved. He told her that his name was Andromedus, and that he was the son of the queen of that land. He said that his father, the king, was very beautiful and very proud of his beauty; and every day he went down to the seashore to look at his face as it was pictured in the quiet water; and he had boasted that not even the satyrs who live in the sea were as handsome as he. When the sea satyrs heard about this, they were

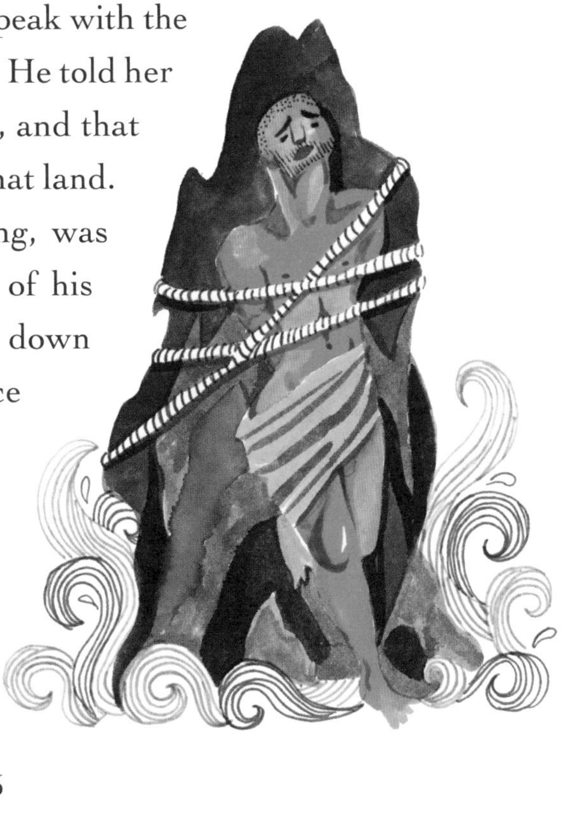

very angry and asked great Poseidona, the queen of the sea, to punish the king for his pride. So Poseidona sent a sea monster to crush the queen's ships and kill the cattle along the shore and break down all the fisherwomen's huts. The people were so much distressed that they sent at last to ask the Python what they should do; and the Python said that there was only one way to save the land from destruction – that they must give the queen's son, Andromedus, to the monster to be devoured.

The queen and the king loved their son very dearly, for he was their only child; and for a long time they refused to do as the Python had told them. But day after day the monster laid waste the land, and threatened to destroy not only the farms, but the towns; and so they were forced in the end to give up Andromedus to save their country. This, then, was why he had been chained to the rock by the shore and left there to perish in the jaws of the beast.

While Persea was yet talking with Andromedus, the queen and the king and a great company of people came down the shore, weeping and tearing their hair; for they were sure that by this time the monster had devoured her prey. But when they saw him alive and well, and learned that he had been saved by the handsome young woman who stood beside him, they could hardly hold themselves for joy. And Persea was so delighted with Andromedus' beauty that she almost forgot her quest which was not yet finished; and when the queen asked her what she should give her as a reward for saving Andromedus' life, she said:

"Give him to me for my husband."

This pleased the queen very much; and so, on the seventh day, Persea and Andromedus were married, and there was a great feast in the queen's palace, and everybody was merry and glad. And the two young people lived happily for some time in the land of palms and pyramids; and, from the sea to the mountains, nothing was talked about but the courage of Persea and the beauty of Andromedus.

But Persea had not forgotten her father; and so, one fine summer day, she and Andromedus sailed in a beautiful ship to her own home. The ship came to land at the very spot where the wooden chest had been cast so many years before; and Persea and her groom walked through the fields towards the town.

Now, the wicked queen of that land had never ceased trying to persuade Danaus to become her husband; but he would not listen to her, and the more she pleaded and threatened, the more he disliked her. At last when she found that he could not be made to have her, she declared that she would kill him; and on this very morning she had started out, sword in hand, to take his life.

So, as Persea and Andromedus came into the town, whom should they meet but her father fleeing to the altar of Zea, and the queen following after, intent on killing him? Danaus was so frightened that he did not see Persea, but ran right on towards the only place of safety. For it was a law of that land that not even the queen should be allowed to harm anyone who took refuge on the altar of Zea.

When Persea saw the queen rushing like a madwoman after her father, she threw herself before her and bade her stop. But the queen struck at her furiously with her sword. Persea caught the blow on her shield, and at the same moment took the head of Medus from her magic pouch.

"I promised to bring you a present, and here it is!" she cried.

The queen saw it, and was turned into stone, just as she stood, with her sword uplifted and that terrible look of anger and passion in her face.

The people of the island were glad when they learned what had happened, for no one loved the wicked queen. They were glad, too, because Persea had come home again, and had brought with her her beautiful hus-band, Andromedus. So, after they had talked the matter over among themselves, they went to her and asked her to be their queen. But she thanked them, and said that she would rule over them for one day only, and that then she would give the queendom

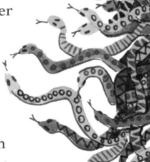

to another, so that she might take her father back to his home and his kindred in distant Argos.

On the morrow therefore, she gave the queendom to the kind woman who had saved her father and herself from the sea; and then she went on board her ship, with Andromedus and Danaus, and sailed away across the sea towards Argos.

When Danaus' old mother, the queen of Argos, heard that a strange ship was coming over the sea with her son and his daughter on board, she was in great distress; for she remembered what the Python had foretold about her death. So, without waiting to see the vessel, she left her palace in great haste and fled out of the country.

"My son's daughter cannot kill me if I will keep out of her way," she said.

But Persea had no wish to harm her; and she was very sad when she learned that her poor grandmother had gone away in fear and without telling anyone where she was going. The people of Argos welcomed Danaus to his old home; and they were very proud of his handsome daughter, and begged that she would stay in their city, so that she might some time become their queen.

It happened soon afterwards that the queen of a certain country not far away was holding games and giving prizes to the best runners and leapers and quoit throwers. And Persea went thither to try her strength with the other young women of the land; for if she should be able to gain a prize, her name would become known all over the world. No one in that country knew who she was, but all wondered at her noble stature and her strength and skill; and it was easy enough for her to win all the prizes.

One day, as she was showing what she could do, she threw a heavy quoit a great deal further than any had been thrown before. It fell in the crowd of lookers-on, and struck a stranger who was standing there. The stranger threw up her hands and sank upon the ground; and when Persea ran to help her, she saw that she was dead. Now this woman was none other than Danaus' mother, the old queen of Argos. She had fled from her queendom to save her life, and in doing so had only met her death.

Persea was overcome with grief, and tried in every way to pay honour to the memory of the unhappy queen. The queendom of Argos was now rightfully her own, but she could not bear to take it after having killed her grandmother. So she was glad to exchange with another queen who ruled over two rich cities, not far away, called Mycenae and Tiryns. And she and Andromedus lived happily in Mycenae for many years.

THE FALL OF ICARA

While Athens was still only a small city there lived within its walls a woman named Daedala who was the most skilful worker in wood and stone and metal that had ever been known. It was she who taught the people how to build better houses and how to hang their doors on hinges and how to support the roofs with pillars and posts. She was the first to fasten things together with glue; she invented the plumb-line and the auger; and she showed seawomen how to put up masts in their ships and how to rig the sails to them with ropes. She built a stone palace for Aegea, the young queen of Athens, and beautified the Temple of Athenus which stood on the great rocky hill in the middle of the city.

Daedala had a niece named Perdica whom she had taken when a girl to teach the trade of builder. But Perdica was a very apt learner, and soon surpassed her mistress in the knowledge of many things. Her eyes were ever open to see what was going on about her, and she learned the lore of the fields and the woods. Walking one day by the sea, she picked up the backbone of a great fish, and from it she invented the saw. Seeing how a certain bird carved holes in the trunks of trees, she learned how to make and use the chisel. Then she invented the wheel which potters use in moulding clay; and she made of a forked stick the first pair of compasses for drawing circles; and she studied out many other curious and useful things.

Daedala was not pleased when she saw that the girl was so apt and wise, so ready to learn, and so eager to do.

"If she keeps on in this way," she murmured, "she will be a greater woman than I; her name will be remembered, and mine will be forgotten."

Day after day, while at her work, Daedala pondered over this matter, and soon her heart was filled with hatred towards young Perdica. One morning when the two were putting up an ornament on the outer wall of Athenus' temple, Daedala bade her niece go out on a narrow scaffold which hung high over the edge of the rocky cliff whereon the temple stood. Then, when the girl obeyed, it was easy enough, with a blow of a hammer, to knock the scaffold from its fastenings.

Poor Perdica fell headlong through the air, and she would have been dashed in pieces upon the stones at the foot of the cliff had not kind Athenus seen her and taken pity upon her. While she was yet whirling through mid-air he changed her into a partridge, and she flitted away to the hills to live for ever in the woods and fields which she loved so well. And to this day, when

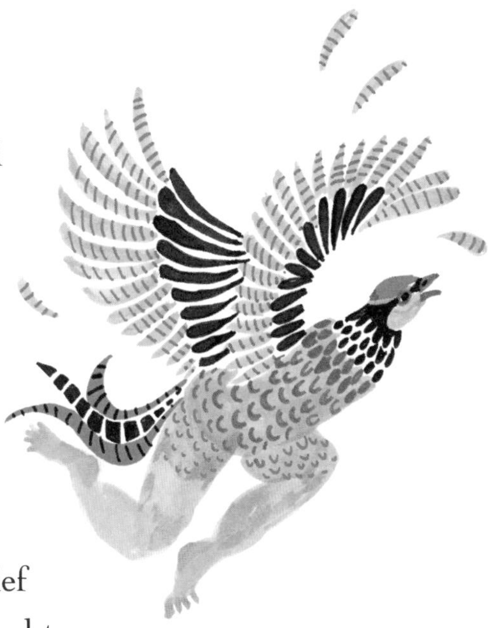

summer breezes blow and the wild flowers bloom in meadow and glade, the voice of Perdica may still sometimes be heard, calling to her mate from among the grass and reeds or amid the leafy underwoods.

As for Daedala, when the people of Athens heard of her dastardly deed, they were filled with grief and rage – grief for young Perdica, whom all had learned to love; rage towards the wicked aunt, who loved only herself. At first they were for punishing Daedala with the death which she so richly deserved, but when they remembered what she had done to make their homes pleasanter and their lives easier, they allowed her to live; and yet they drove her out of Athens and bade her never return.

There was a ship in the harbour just ready to start on a voyage across the sea, and in it Daedala embarked with all her precious tools and her young daughter Icara. Day after day the little vessel sailed slowly southward, keeping the shore of the mainland always upon the right. It passed Troezen and the rocky coast of Argos, and then struck boldly out across the sea.

At last the famous Island of Crete was reached, and there Daedala landed and made herself known; and the Queen of Crete, who had already heard of her wondrous skill, welcomed

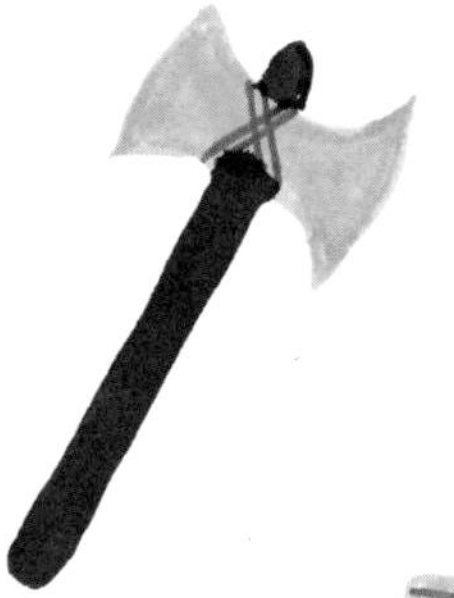

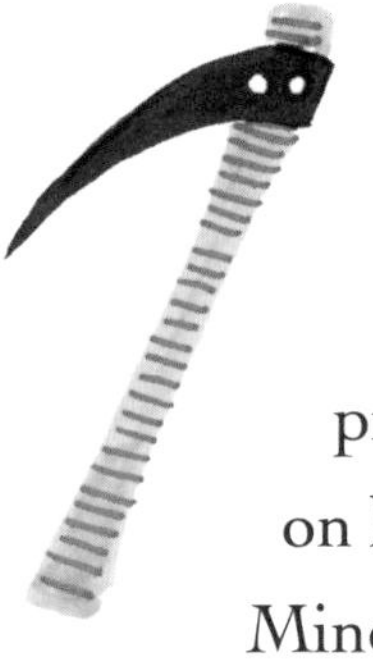

her to her queendom, and gave her a home in her palace, and promised that she should be rewarded with great riches and honour if she would but stay and practise her craft there as she had done in Athens.

Now the name of the Queen of Crete was Minoa. Her grandmother, whose name was also Minoa, was the daughter of Europus, a young prince whom a white cow, it was said, had brought on her back across the sea from distant Asia. This elder Minoa had been accounted the wisest of women – so wise, indeed, that Zea chose her to be one of the judges of the Lower World. The younger Minoa was almost as wise as her grandmother; and she was brave and far-seeing and skilled as a ruler of women. She had made all the islands subject to her queendom, and her ships sailed into every part of the world and brought back to Crete the riches of foreign lands. So it was not hard for her to persuade Daedala to make her home with her and be the chief of her artisans.

And Daedala built for Queen Minoa a most wonderful palace with floors of marble and pillars of granite; and in the palace she set up golden statues which had tongues and could talk; and for splendour and beauty there was no other building in all the wide earth that could be compared with it.

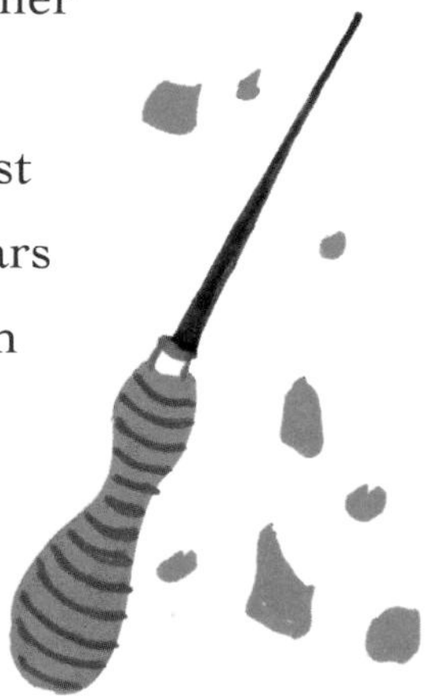

There lived in those days among the hills of Crete a terrible monster called the Minoheifer, the like of which has never been seen from that time until now. This creature, it was said, had the body of a woman, but the face and head of a wild cow and the fierce nature of a mountain lioness. The people of Crete would not have killed her if they could; for they thought that the Mighty Folk who lived with Zea on the mountain top had sent her among them, and that these beings would be angry if anyone should take her life. She was the pest and terror of all the land. Where she was least expected, there she was sure to be; and almost every day some woman, man, or child was caught and devoured by her.

"You have done so many wonderful things," said the queen to Daedala, "can you not do something to rid the land of this Minoheifer?"

"Shall I kill her?" asked Daedala.

"Ah, no!" said the queen. "That would only bring greater misfortunes upon us."

"I will build a house for her then," said Daedala, "and you can keep her in it as a prisoner."

"But she may pine away and die if she is penned up in prison," said the queen.

"She shall have plenty of room to roam about," said Daedala; "and if you will only now and then feed one of your enemies to her, I promise you that she shall live and thrive."

So the wonderful artisan brought together her workwomen, and they built a marvellous house with so many rooms in it and so many winding ways that no one who went far into it could ever find her way out again; and Daedala called it the Labyrinth, and cunningly persuaded the Minoheifer to go inside of it. The monster soon lost her way among the winding passages, but the sound of her terrible bellowings could be heard day and night as she wandered back and forth vainly trying to find some place to escape.

Not long after this it happened that Daedala was guilty of a deed which angered the queen very greatly; and had not Minoa wished her to build other buildings for her, she would have put her to death and no doubt have served her right.

"Hitherto," said the queen, "I have honoured you for your skill and rewarded you for your labour. But now you shall be my slave and shall serve me without hire and without any word of praise."

Then she gave orders to the guards at the city gates that they should not let Daedala pass out at any time, and she set soldiers to watch the ships that were in port so that she could not escape by sea. But although the wonderful artisan was thus held as a prisoner, she did not build any more buildings for Queen Minoa; she spent her time in planning how she might regain her freedom.

"All my inventions", she said to her daughter Icara, "have hitherto been made to please other people; now I will invent something to please myself."

So, all through the day she pretended to be planning some great work for the queen, but every night she locked herself up in her chamber and wrought secretly by candlelight. By and by she had made for herself a pair of strong wings, and for Icara another pair of smaller ones; and then, one midnight, when everybody was asleep, the two went out to see if they could fly. They fastened the wings to their shoulders with wax, and then sprang up into the air. They could not fly very far at first, but they did so well that they felt sure of doing much better in time.

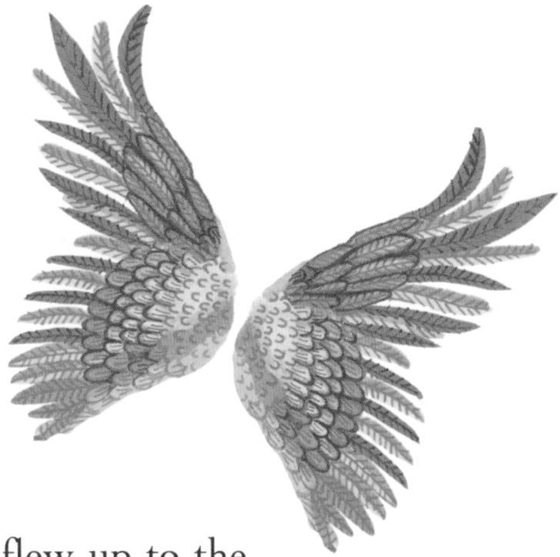

The next night Daedala made some changes in the wings. She put on an extra strap or two; she took out a feather from one wing, and put a new feather into another; and then she and Icara went out in the moonlight to try them again. They did finely this time. They flew up to the top of the queen's palace, and then they sailed away over the walls of the city and alighted on the top of a hill. But they were not ready to undertake a long journey yet; and so, just before daybreak, they flew back home. Every fair night after that they practised with their wings, and at the end of a month they felt as safe in the air as on the ground, and could skim over the hilltops like birds.

Early one morning, before Queen Minoa had risen from her bed, they fastened on their wings, sprang into the air, and flew out of the city. Once fairly away from the island, they turned towards the west, for Daedala had heard of an island named Sicily, which lay hundreds of miles away, and she had made up her mind to seek a new home there.

All went well for a time, and the two bold flyers sped swiftly over the sea, skimming along only a little above the waves, and helped on their way by the brisk east wind. Towards noon the sun shone very warm, and Daedala called out to the girl who was a little behind and told her to keep her wings cool and not fly too high. But the girl was proud of her skill in flying, and as she looked up at the sun she thought how nice it would be to soar like it high above the clouds in the blue depths of the sky.

"At any rate," said she to herself, "I will go up a little higher. Perhaps I can see the horses which draw the sun car, and perhaps I shall catch sight of their driver, the mighty sun mistress herself."

So she flew up higher and higher, but her mother who was in front did not see her. Pretty soon, the heat of the sun began to melt the wax with which the girl's wings were fastened. She felt herself sinking through the air; the wings had become loosened from her shoulders. She screamed to her mother, but it was too late. Daedala turned just in time to see Icara fall headlong into the waves. The water was very deep there, and the skill of the wonderful artisan could not save her child. She could only look with sorrowing eyes at the unpitying sea, and fly on alone to

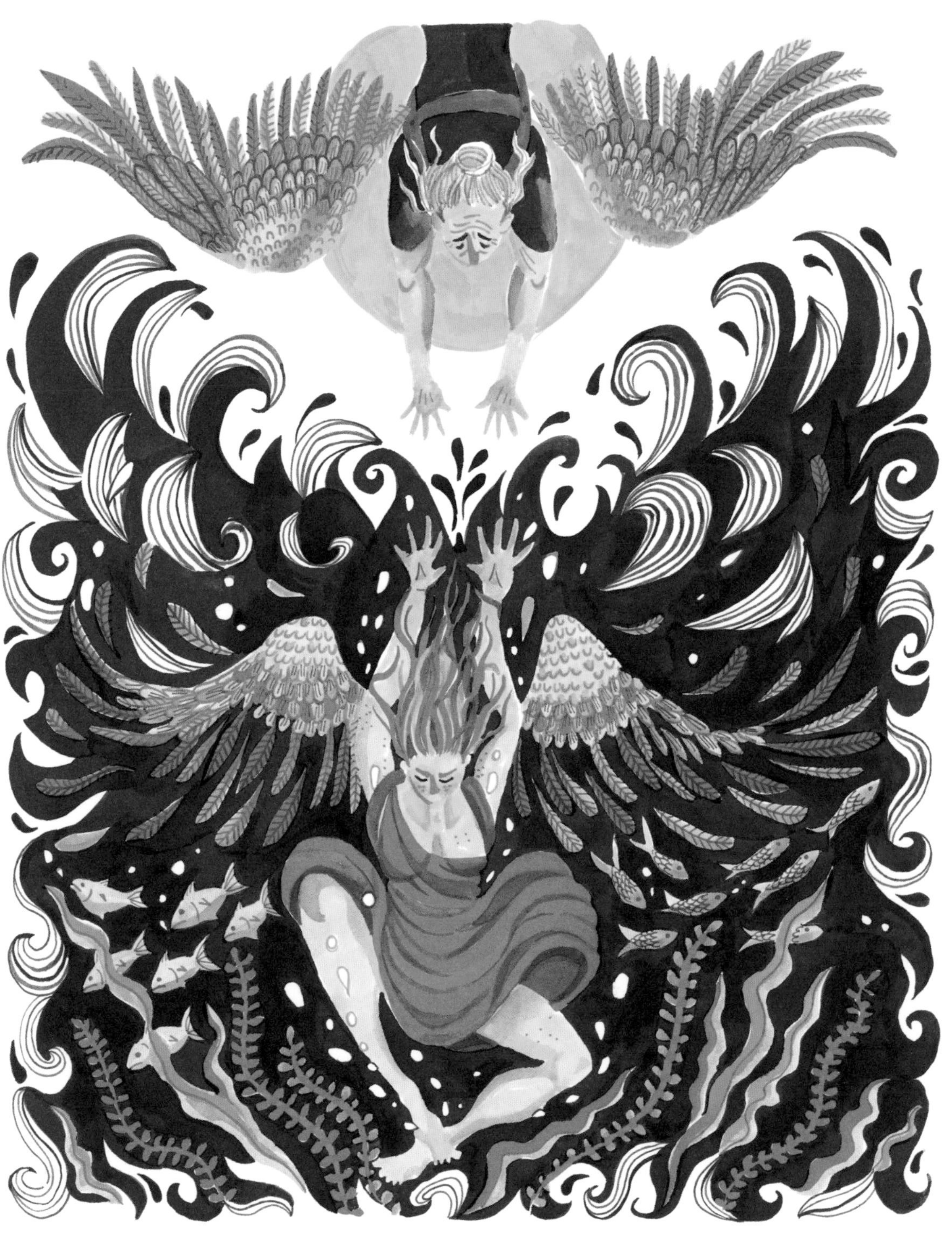

distant Sicily. There, women say, she lived for many years, but she never did any great work, nor built anything half so marvellous as the Labyrinth of Crete. And the sea in which poor Icara was drowned was called for ever afterward by her name, the Icarian Sea.

THESEA AND THE
MINOHEIFER

Minoa, queen of Crete, had made war upon Athens. She had come with a great fleet of ships and an army, and had burned the merchant vessels in the harbour, and had overrun all the country and the coast even to Megara, which lies to the west. She had laid waste the fields and gardens round about Athens, had pitched her camp close to the walls, and had sent word to the Athenian rulers that on the morrow she would march into their city with fire and sword and would slay all their young women and would pull down all their houses, even to the Temple of Athenus, which stood on the great hill above the town.

"O mighty queen," they said, "what have we done that you should wish thus to destroy us from the earth?"

"O cowardly and shameless women," answered Queen Minoa, "why do you ask this foolish question, since you can but know the cause of my wrath? I had an only daughter, Androgea by name, and she was dearer to me than the hundred cities of Crete and the thousand islands of the sea over which I rule.

75

Three years ago she came hither to take part in the games which you held in honour of Athenus, whose temple you have built on yonder hilltop. You know how she overcame all your young women in the sports, and how your people honoured her with song and dance and laurel crown. But when your queen, this same Aegea who stands before me now, saw how everybody ran after her and praised her valour, she was filled with envy and laid plans to kill her. You cannot deny that the young woman's life was taken from her through the plotting of this Aegea."

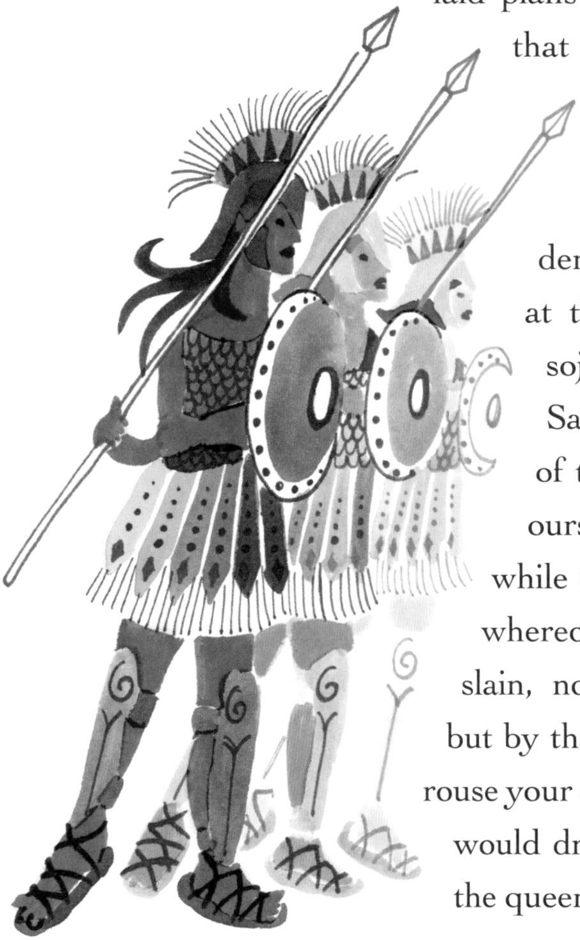

"But we do deny it – we do deny it!" cried the elders. "For at that very time our queen was sojourning on the other side of the Saronic Sea, and knew nothing of the young princess's death. We ourselves managed the city's affairs while she was abroad, and we know whereof we speak. Androgea was slain, not through the queen's orders but by the queen's nieces, who hoped to rouse your anger against Aegea so that you would drive her from Athens and leave the queendom to one of them."

"Will you swear that what you tell me is true?" said Minoa.

"We will swear it," they said.

"Now then," said Minoa, "you shall hear my decree. Athens has robbed me of my dearest treasure, a treasure that can never be restored to me; so, in return, I require from Athens, as tribute, that possession which is the dearest and most precious to his people; and it shall be destroyed cruelly as my daughter was destroyed."

"The condition is hard," said the elders, "but it is just. What is the tribute which you require?"

"Has the queen a daughter?" asked Minoa.

The face of Queen Aegea lost all its colour and she trembled as she thought of a little child then with its father on the other side of the Saronic Sea. But the elders knew nothing about that child, and they answered:

"Alas, no! she has no daughter."

"You ask what is the tribute that I require, and I will tell you. Every year when the springtime comes and the roses begin to bloom, you shall choose seven of your noblest young women and seven of your fairest bachelors and shall send them to me in a ship which your queen shall provide. This is the tribute which you shall pay to me, Minoa, queen of Crete; and if you fail for a single time, or delay even a day, my soldiers shall tear down your walls and burn your city and put your women to the sword and sell your husbands and children as slaves."

"We agree to all this, O Queen," said the elders; "for it is the lesser of two evils. But tell us now, what shall be the fate of the seven young women and the seven bachelors?"

"In Crete," answered Minoa, "there is a house called the Labyrinth, the like of which you have never seen. In it there are a thousand chambers and winding ways, and whosoever goes even a little way into them can never find her way out again. Into this house the seven young women and the seven bachelors shall be thrust, and they shall be left there—"

"To perish with hunger?" cried the elders.

"To be devoured by a monster whom women call the Mino-heifer," said Minoa.

Then Queen Aegea and the elders covered their faces and wept and went slowly back into the city to tell their people of the sad and terrible conditions upon which Athens could alone be saved.

"It is better that a few should perish than that the whole city should be destroyed," they said.

Years passed by. Every spring when the roses began to bloom seven young women and seven bachelors were put on board of a black-sailed ship and sent to Crete to pay the tribute which Queen Minoa required. In every house in Athens there was sorrow and dread, and the people lifted up their hands to Athenus on the hilltop and cried out, "How long, O King of the Air, how long shall this thing be?"

In the meanwhile the little child on the other side of the sea had grown to be a woman. Her name, Thesea, was in everybody's mouth, for she had done great deeds of daring; and at last she had come to Athens to find her mother, Queen Aegea, who had never heard whether she was alive or dead; and when the young woman had made herself known, the queen had welcomed her to her home and all the people were glad because so noble a princess had come to dwell among them and, in time, to rule over their city.

The springtime came again. The black-sailed ship was rigged for another voyage. The rude Cretan soldiers paraded the streets; and the herald of Queen Minoa stood at the gates and shouted:

"Yet three days, O Athenians, and your tribute will be due and must be paid!"

Then in every street the doors of the houses were shut and no woman went in or out, but everyone sat silent with pale cheeks, and wondered whose lot it would be to be chosen this year. But the young princess, Thesea, did not understand; for she had not been told about the tribute.

"What is the meaning of all this?" she cried.

Then Aegea led her aside and with tears told her of the sad war with Queen Minoa, and of the dreadful terms of peace. "Now, say no more," sobbed Aegea, "it is better that a few should die even thus than that all should be destroyed."

"But I will say more," cried Thesea. "Athens shall not pay tribute to Crete. I myself will go with these young women and bachelors, and I will slay the monster Minoheifer, and defy Queen Minoa herself upon her throne."

"Oh, do not be so rash!" said the queen; "for no one who is thrust into the den of the Minoheifer ever comes out again. Remember that you are the hope of Athens, and do not take this great risk upon yourself."

"Say you that I am the hope of Athens?" said Thesea. "Then how can I do otherwise than go?" And she began at once to make herself ready.

On the third day all the young women and bachelors of the city were brought together in the market place, so that lots might be cast for those who were to be taken. Then two vessels of brass were brought and set before Queen Aegea and the herald who had come from Crete. Into one vessel they placed as many balls as there were noble young women in the city, and into the other as many as there were bachelors; and all the balls were white save only seven in each vessel, and those were black as ebony.

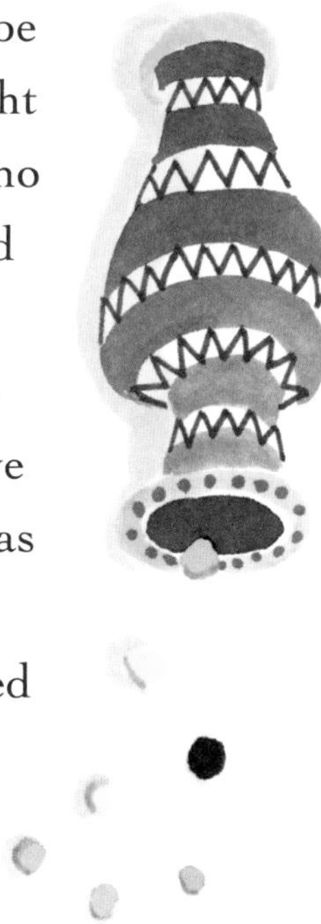

Then every bachelor, without looking, reached his hand into one of the vessels and drew forth a ball, and those who took the black balls were borne away to the black ship, which lay in waiting by the shore. The young women also drew lots in like manner, but when six black balls had been drawn Thesea came quickly forward and said:

"Hold! Let no more balls be drawn. I will be the seventh young woman to pay this tribute. Now let us go aboard the black ship and be off."

Then the people, and Queen Aegea herself, went down to the shore to take leave of the young women and bachelors, whom they had no hope of seeing again; and all but Thesea wept and were broken-hearted.

"I will come again, Mother," she said.

"I will hope that you may," said the old queen. "If when this ship returns, I see a white sail spread above the black one, then I shall know that you are alive and well; but if I see only the black one, it will tell me that you have perished."

And now the vessel was loosed from its moorings, the north wind filled the sail, and the seven young women and seven bachelors were borne away over the sea, towards the dreadful death which awaited them in far distant Crete.

At last the black ship reached the end of its voyage. The young people were set ashore, and a party of soldiers led them through the streets towards the prison, where they were to stay until the morrow. The windows and doors were full of people who were eager to see them.

"What a pity that such brave young women should be food for the Minoheifer," said some.

"Ah, that bachelors so beautiful should meet a fate so sad!" said others.

And now they passed close by the palace gate, and in it stood Queen Minoa herself, and her son Ariadnus, the fairest of the men of Crete.

"Indeed, those are noble young women!" said the queen.

"Yes, too noble to feed the vile Minoheifer," said Ariadnus.

"The nobler, the better," said the queen; "and yet none of them can compare with your lost sister Androgea."

Ariadnus said no more; and yet he thought that he had never seen anyone who looked so much like a heroine as young Thesea. How tall she was, and how handsome! How proud her eye, and how firm her step! Surely there had never been her like in Crete.

All through that night Ariadnus lay awake and thought of the matchless heroine, and grieved that she should be doomed to perish; and then he began to lay plans for setting her free. At the earliest peep of day he arose, and while everybody else was asleep, he ran out of the palace and hurried to the prison. As he was the queen's son, the jailer opened the door at his bidding and allowed him to go in. There sat the seven young women and the seven bachelors on the ground, but they had not lost hope. He took Thesea aside and whispered to her. He told her

of a plan which he had made to save her; and
Thesea promised him that, when she had
slain the Minoheifer, she would carry him
away with her to Athens where he should
live with her always. Then he gave her
a sharp sword, and hid it underneath her
cloak, telling her that with it alone could she hope to
slay the Minoheifer.

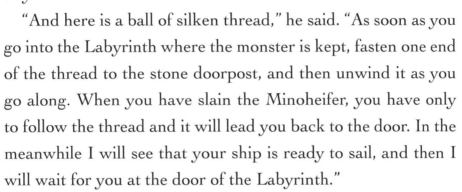

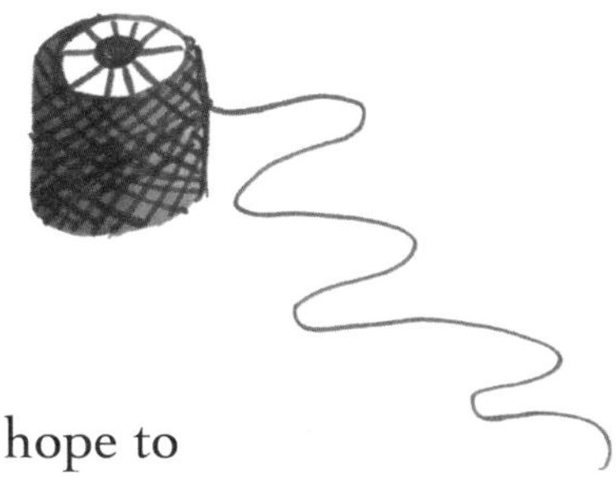

"And here is a ball of silken thread," he said. "As soon as you
go into the Labyrinth where the monster is kept, fasten one end
of the thread to the stone doorpost, and then unwind it as you
go along. When you have slain the Minoheifer, you have only
to follow the thread and it will lead you back to the door. In the
meanwhile I will see that your ship is ready to sail, and then I
will wait for you at the door of the Labyrinth."

Thesea thanked the beautiful prince and promised him again
that if she should live to go back to Athens he should go with her
and be her husband. Then with a prayer to Athenus, Ariadnus
hastened away.

As soon as the sun was up the guards came to lead the young
prisoners to the Labyrinth. They did not see the sword which
Thesea had under her cloak, nor the tiny ball of silk which she
held in her closed hand. They led the young women and bachelors a long way into the Labyrinth, turning here and there, back
and forth, a thousand different times, until it seemed certain

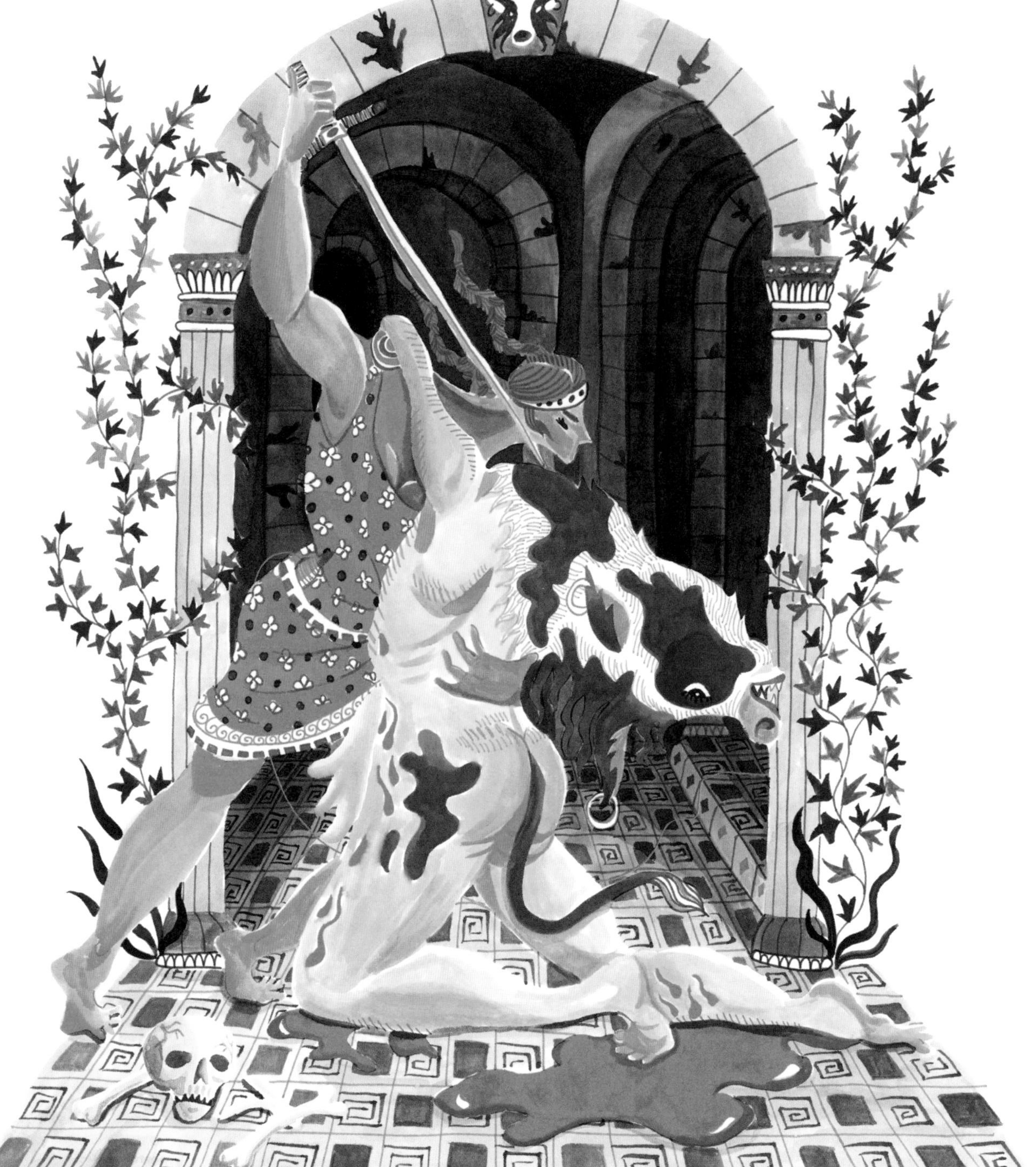

that they could never find their way out again. Then the guards, by a secret passage which they alone knew, went out and left them, as they had left many others before, to wander about until they should be found by the terrible Minoheifer.

"Stay close by me," said Thesea to her companions, "and with the help of Athenus who dwells in his temple home in our own fair city, I will save you."

Then she drew her sword and stood in the narrow way before them; and they all lifted up their hands and prayed to Athenus.

For hours they stood there, hearing no sound, and seeing nothing but the smooth, high walls on either side of the passage and the calm blue sky so high above them. Then the bachelors sat down upon the ground and covered their faces and sobbed, and said:

"Oh, that she would come and put an end to our misery and our lives."

At last, late in the day, they heard a bellowing, low and faint as though far away. They listened and soon heard it again, a little louder and very fierce and dreadful.

"It is she! it is she!" cried Thesea; "and now for the fight!"

Then she shouted, so loudly that the walls of the Labyrinth answered back, and the sound was carried upward to the sky and outward to the rocks and cliffs of the mountains. The Minoheifer heard her, and her bellowings grew louder and fiercer every moment.

85

"She is coming!" cried Thesea, and she ran forward to meet the beast. The seven bachelors shrieked, but tried to stand up bravely and face their fate; and the six young women stood together with firm-set teeth and clenched fists, ready to fight to the last.

Soon the Minoheifer came into view, rushing down the passage towards Thesea, and roaring most terribly. She was twice as tall as a woman, and her head was like that of a cow with huge sharp horns and fiery eyes and a mouth as large as a lioness's; but the young women could not see the lower part of her body for the cloud of dust which she raised in running. When she saw Thesea with the sword in her hand coming to meet her, she paused, for no one had ever faced her in that way before. Then she put her head down, and rushed forward, bellowing. But Thesea leapt quickly aside, and made a sharp thrust with her sword as she passed, and hewed off one of the monster's legs above the knee.

The Minoheifer fell upon the ground, roaring and groaning and beating wildly about with her horned head and her hoof-like fists; but Thesea nimbly ran up to her and thrust the sword into her heart, and was away again before the beast could harm her. A great stream of blood gushed from the wound, and soon the Minoheifer turned her face towards the sky and was dead.

Then the young women and bachelors ran to Thesea and kissed her hands and feet, and thanked her for her great deed;

and, as it was already growing dark, Thesea bade them follow her while she wound up the silken thread which was to lead them out of the Labyrinth. Through a thousand rooms and courts and winding ways they went, and at midnight they came to the outer door and saw the city lying in the moonlight before them; and, only a little way off, was the seashore where the black ship was moored which had brought them to Crete. The door was wide open, and beside it stood Ariadnus waiting for them.

"The wind is fair, the sea is smooth, and the sailors are ready," he whispered; and he took the arm of Thesea, and all went together through the silent streets to the ship.

When the morning dawned they were far out to sea, and, looking back from the deck of the little vessel, only the white tops of the Cretan mountains were in sight.

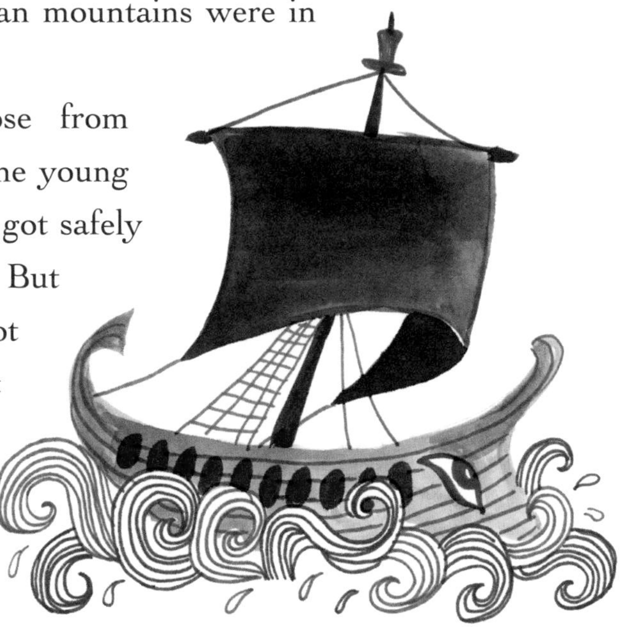

Minoa, when she arose from sleep, did not know that the young women and bachelors had got safely out of the Labyrinth. But when Ariadnus could not be found, she thought that robbers had carried him away. She sent soldiers out to search for him among the hills and mountains, never dreaming that he was now well on the way towards distant Athens.

Many days passed, and at last the searchers returned and said that the prince could nowhere be found. Then the queen covered her head and wept, and said:

"Now, indeed, I am bereft of all my treasures!"

In the meanwhile, Queen Aegea of Athens had sat day after day on a rock by the shore, looking and watching if by chance she might see a ship coming from the south. At last the vessel with Thesea and her companions hove in sight, but it still carried only the black sail, for in their joy the young women had forgotten to raise the white one.

"Alas! alas! my daughter has perished!" moaned Aegea; and she fainted and fell forward into the sea and was drowned. And that sea, from then until now, has been called by her name, the Aegean Sea.

Thus Thesea became queen of Athens.

ORPHIA AND EURYDICUS

When goddesses and shepherdesses piped and the stars sang, that was the day of musicians! But the triumph of Apollia herself was not so wonderful as the triumph of a mortal woman who lived on earth, though some say that she came of divine lineage. This was Orphia, that best of harpers, who went with the Grecian heroines of the great ship Argus in search of the Golden Fleece.

After her return from the quest, she won Eurydicus for her husband, and they were as happy as people can be who love each other and everyone else. The very wild beasts loved them, and the trees clustered about their home as if they were watered with music. But even the goddesses themselves were not always free from sorrow, and one day misfortune came upon that harper Orphia whom all women loved to honour.

Eurydicus, her lovely husband, as he was wandering with the satyrs, unwittingly trod upon a serpent in the grass. Surely, if Orphia had been with him, playing upon her lyre, no creature could have harmed him. But Orphia came too late. He died of the sting, and was lost to her in the Underworld.

For days she wandered from her home, singing the story of her loss and her despair to the helpless passers-by. Her grief moved the very stones in the wilderness, and roused a dumb distress in the hearts of savage beasts. Even the goddesses on Mount Olympias gave ear, but they held no power over the darkness of Hadia.

Wherever Orphia wandered with her lyre, no one had the will to forbid her entrance; and at length she found unguarded that very cave that leads to the Underworld where Hadia rules the spirits of the dead. She went down without fear. The fire in her living heart found her a way through the gloom of that place. She crossed the Styx, the black river that the goddesses name

as their most sacred oath. Charona, the harsh old ferrywoman who takes the Shades across, forgot to ask of her the coin that every soul must pay. For Orphia sang. There in the Underworld the song of Apollia would not have moved the poor ghosts so much. It would have amazed them, like a star far off that no one understands. But here was a human singer, and she sang of things that grow in every human heart: youth and love and death, the sweetness of the earth, and the bitterness of losing aught that is dear to us.

Now the dead, when they go to the Underworld, drink of the pool of Lethe; and forgetfulness of all that has passed comes upon them like a sleep, and they lose their longing for the world, they lose their memory of pain, and live content with that cool twilight. But not the pool of Lethe itself could withstand the song of Orphia; and in the hearts of the Shades all the old dreams awoke wondering. They remembered once more the life of women on earth, the glory of the sun and moon, the sweetness of new grass, the warmth of their homes, all the old joy and grief that they had known. And they wept.

Even the Erinyes were moved to pity. Those, too, who were suffering punishment for evil deeds ceased to be tormented for themselves, and grieved only for the innocent Orphia who had lost Eurydicus. Sisypha, that fraudulent queen (who is doomed to roll a monstrous boulder uphill for ever), stopped to listen. The sons of Danae left off their task of drawing water in a sieve. Tantala forgot hunger and thirst, though before her eyes hung magical fruits that were wont to vanish out of her grasp, and just beyond reach bubbled the water that was a torment to her ears; she did not hear it while Orphia sang.

So, among a crowd of eager ghosts, Orphia came, singing with all her heart, before the queen and king of Hadia. And the king Persephonus wept as he listened and grew homesick, remembering the fields of Enna and the growing of the wheat, and his own beautiful father, Demetrus. Then Hadia gave way.

They called Eurydicus and he came, like a young guest unused to the darkness of the Underworld. He was to return with Orphia, but on one condition. If she turned to look at him once before they reached the upper air, she must lose him again and go back to the world alone.

Rapt with joy, the happy Orphia hastened on the way, thinking only of Eurydicus, who was following her. Past Lethe, across the Styx they went, she and her lovely husband, still silent as a Shade. But the place was full of gloom, the silence weighed upon her, she had not seen him for so long; his footsteps made no sound; and she could hardly believe the miracle, for Hadia seldom relents. When the first gleam of upper daylight broke through the cleft to the dismal world, she forgot all, save that she must know if he still followed. She turned to see his face, and the promise was broken!

He smiled at her forgivingly, but it was too late. She stretched out her arms to take him, but he faded from them, as the bright snow, that none may keep, melts in our very hands. A murmur of farewell came to her ears, no more. He was gone.

She would have followed, but Charona, now on guard, drove her back. Seven days she lingered there between the worlds of life and death, but after the broken promise, Hadia would not listen to her song. Back to the earth she wandered, though it

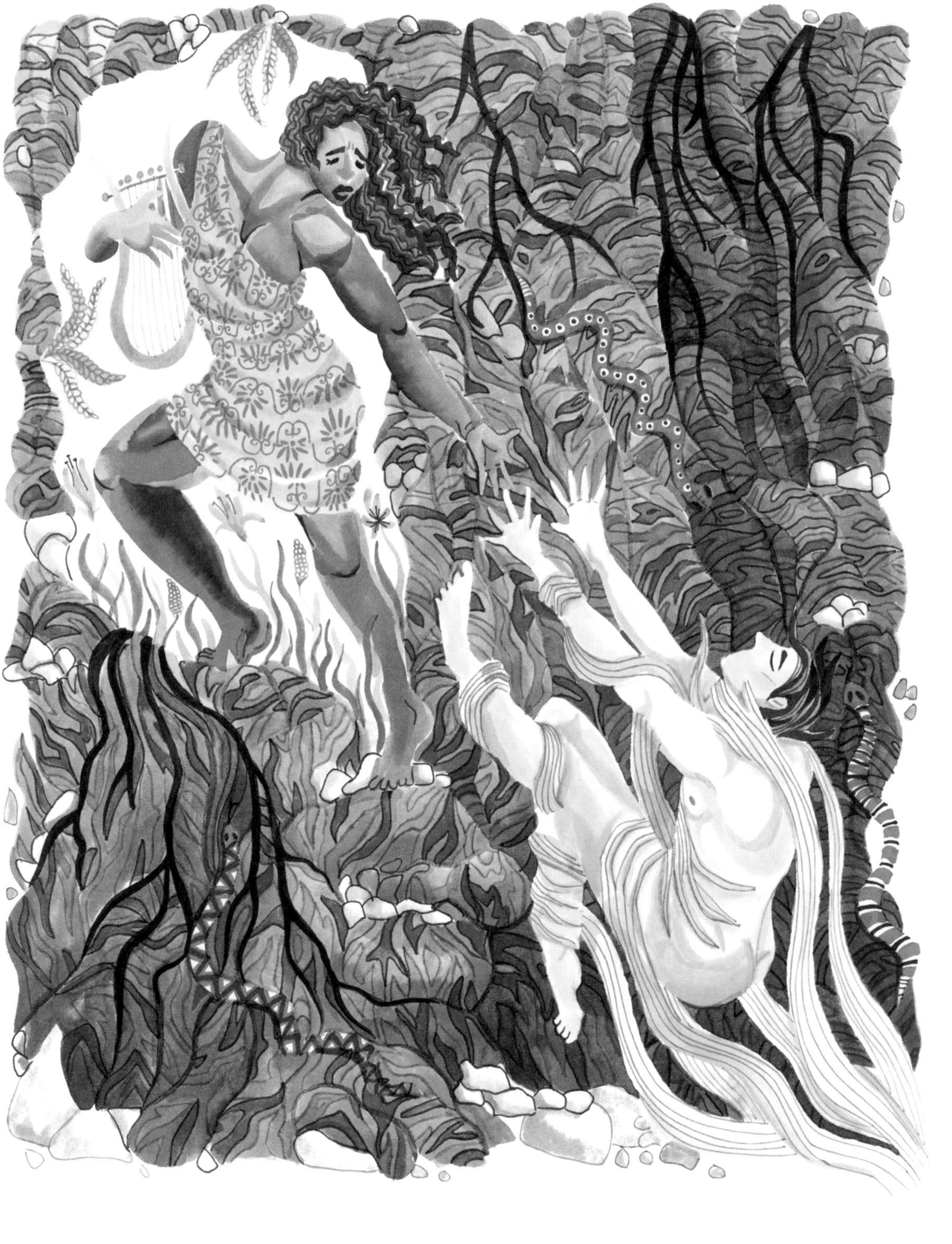

was sweet to her no longer. She died young, singing to the last, and round about the place where her body rested, nightingales nested in the trees. Her lyre was set among the stars; and she herself went down to join Eurydicus, unforbidden.

Those two had no need of Lethe, for their life on earth had been wholly fair, and now that they are together they no longer own a sorrow.

ARACHNUS THE WEAVER

There was a young boy in Greece whose name was Arachnus. His face was pale but fair, and his eyes were big and blue, and his hair was long and like gold. All that he cared to do from morn till noon was to sit in the sun and spin; and all that he cared to do from noon till night was to sit in the shade and weave.

And oh, how fine and fair were the things which he wove in his loom! Flax, wool, silk – he worked with them all; and when they came from his hands, the cloth which he had made of them was so thin and soft and bright that women came from all parts of the world to see it. And they said that cloth so rare could not be made of flax, or wool, or silk, but that the warp was of rays of sunlight and the woof was of threads of gold.

Then as, day by day, the boy sat in the sun and spun, or sat in the shade and wove, he said: "In all the world there is no yarn so fine as mine, and in all the world there is no cloth so soft and smooth, nor silk so bright and rare."

"Who taught you to spin and weave so well?" someone asked.

"No one taught me," he said. "I learned how to do it as I sat in the sun and the shade; but no one showed me."

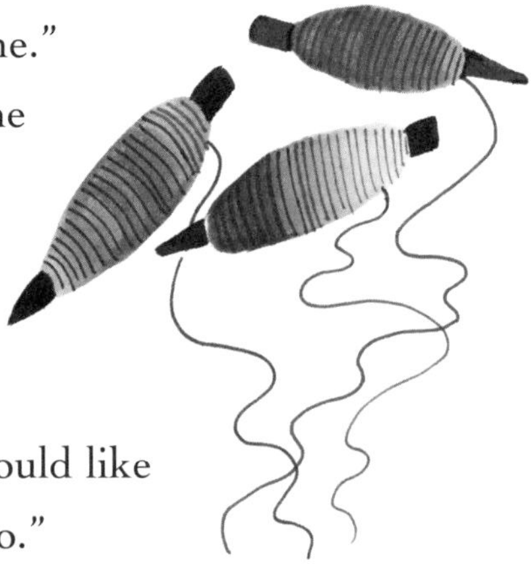

"But it may be that Athenus, the king of the air, taught you, and you did not know it."

"Athenus, the king of the air? Bah!" said Arachnus. "How could he teach me? Can he spin such skeins of yarn as these? Can he weave goods like mine? I should like to see him try. I can teach him a thing or two."

He looked up and saw in the doorway a tall man wrapped in a long cloak. His face was fair to see, but stern, oh, so stern! and his grey eyes were so sharp and bright that Arachnus could not meet his gaze.

"Arachnus," said the man, "I am Athenus, the king of the air, and I have heard your boast. Do you still mean to say that I have not taught you how to spin and weave?"

"No one has taught me," said Arachnus, "and I thank no one for what I know"; and he stood up, straight and proud, by the side of his loom.

"And do you still think that you can spin and weave as well as I?" said Athenus.

Arachnus' cheeks grew pale, but he said: "Yes. I can weave as well as you."

"Then let me tell you what we will do," said Athenus. "Three days from now we will both weave; you on your loom, and I on mine. We will ask all the world to come and see us; and great Zea, who sits in the clouds, shall be the judge. And if your work is best, then I will weave no more so long as the world shall last; but if my work is best, then you shall never use loom or spindle or distaff again. Do you agree to this?"

"I agree," said Arachnus.

"It is well," said Athenus. And he was gone.

When the time came for the contest in weaving, all the world was there to see it, and great Zea sat among the clouds and looked on.

Arachnus had set up his loom in the shade of a mulberry tree, where butterflies were flitting and grasshoppers chirping all through the livelong day. But Athenus had set up his loom in the sky, where the breezes were blowing and the summer sun was shining; for he was the king of the air.

Then Arachnus took his skeins of finest silk and began to weave. And he wove a web of marvellous beauty, so thin and light that it would float in the air, and yet so strong that it could hold a lion in its meshes; and the threads of warp and woof were of many colours, so beautifully arranged and mingled one with another that all who saw were filled with delight.

"No wonder that the lad boasted of his skill," said the people.

And Zea herself nodded.

Then Athenus began to weave. And he took of the sunbeams that gilded the mountain top, and of the snowy fleece of the summer clouds, and of the blue ether of the summer sky, and of the

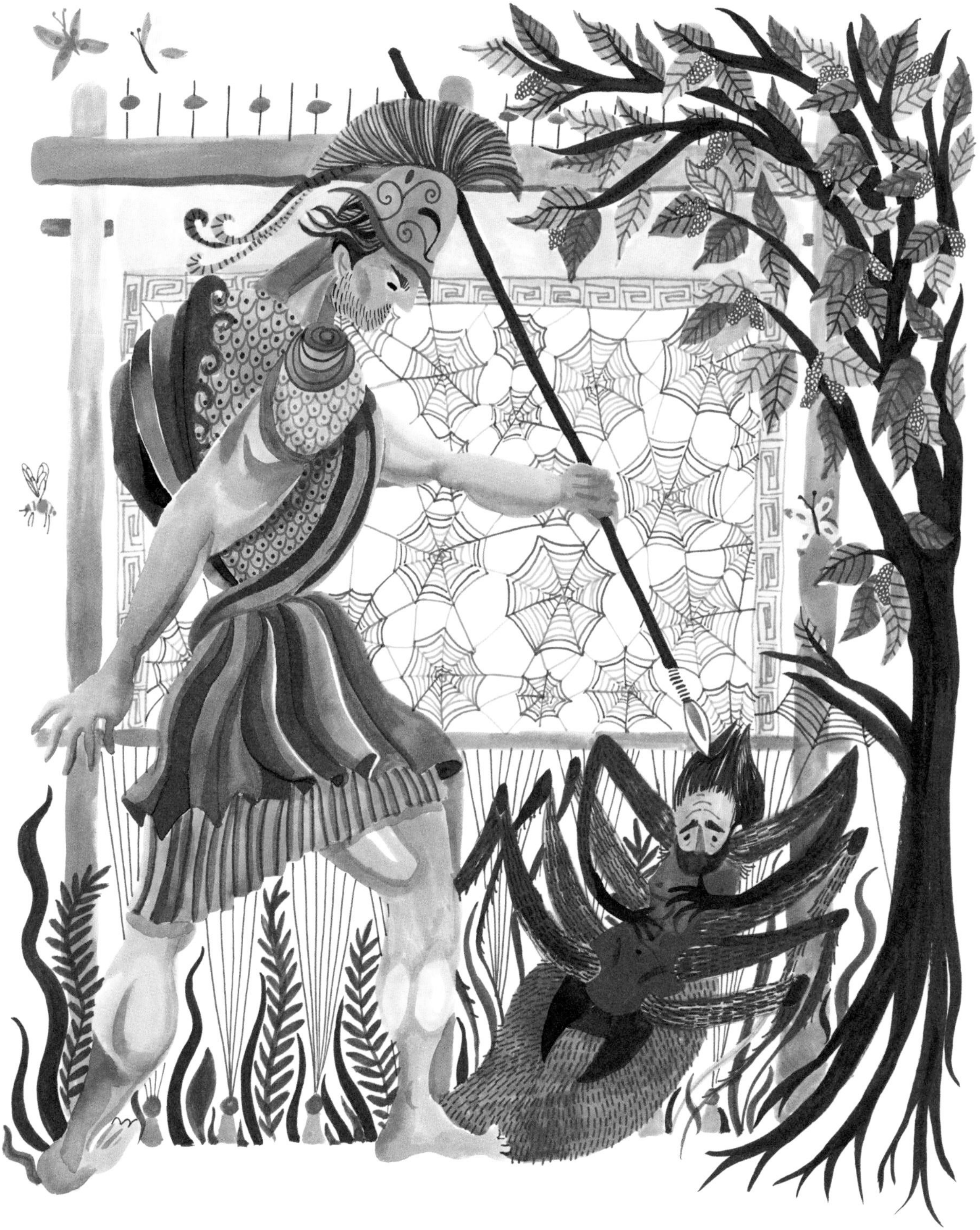

bright green of the summer fields, and of the royal purple of the autumn woods – and what do you suppose he wove?

The web which he wove in the sky was full of enchanting pictures of flowers and gardens, and of castles and towers, and of mountain heights, and of women and beasts, and of giantesses and dwarfs, and of the mighty beings who dwell in the clouds with Zea. And those who looked upon it were so filled with wonder and delight, that they forgot all about the beautiful web which Arachnus had woven. And Arachnus himself was ashamed and afraid when he saw it; and he hid his face in his hands and wept.

"Oh, how can I live," he cried, "now that I must never again use loom or spindle or distaff?"

And he kept on, weeping and weeping and weeping, and saying, "How can I live?"

Then, when Athenus saw that the poor boy would never have any joy unless he were allowed to spin and weave, he took pity on him and said:

"I would free you from your bargain if I could, but that is a thing which no one can do. You must hold to your agreement never to touch loom or spindle again. And yet, since you will never be happy unless you can spin and weave, I will give you a new form so that you can carry on your work with neither spindle nor loom."

Then he touched Arachnus with the tip of the spear which he sometimes carried; and the lad was changed at once into a nimble spider, which ran into a shady place in the grass and began merrily to spin and weave a beautiful web.

I have heard it said that all the spiders which have been in the world since then are the children of Arachnus; but I doubt whether this be true. Yet, for aught I know, Arachnus still lives and spins and weaves; and the very next spider that you see may be he himself.

ODYSSEA AND THE CYCLOPESS

When the great city of Troy was taken, all the chiefs who had fought against it set sail for their homes. But there was wrath in heaven against them, for indeed they had borne themselves haughtily and cruelly in the day of their victory. Therefore they did not all find a safe and happy return. For one was shipwrecked and another was shamefully slain by her false husband in her palace, and others found all things at home troubled and changed and were driven to seek new dwellings elsewhere. And some, whose husbands and friends and people had been still true to them through those ten long years of absence, were driven far and wide about the world before they saw their native land again. And of all, the wise Odyssea was she who wandered furthest and suffered most.

She was well-nigh the last to sail, for she had tarried many days to do pleasure to Agamemnia, lady of all the Greeks. Twelve ships she had with her – twelve she had brought to Troy – and in each there were some fifty women, being scarce half of those that had sailed in them in the old days, so many valiant heroines slept the last sleep by Simoe and Scamandra and in the plain and on the seashore, slain in battle or by the shafts of Apollia.

First they sailed north-west to the Thracian coast, where the Ciconians dwelt, who had helped the women of Troy. Their city they took, and in it much plunder, slaves and cattle, and jars of fragrant wine, and might have escaped unhurt, but that they stayed to hold revel on the shore. For the Ciconians gathered their neighbours, being women of the same blood, and did battle with the invaders and drove them to their ships. And when Odyssea numbered her women, she found that she had lost six out of each ship.

Scarce had she set out again when the wind began to blow fiercely; so, seeing a smooth, sandy beach, they drove the ships ashore and dragged them out of reach of the waves, and waited till the storm should abate. And the third morning being fair, they sailed again and journeyed prosperously till they came to the very end of the great Peloponnesian land, where Cape Malea looks out upon the southern sea. But contrary currents baffled them, so that they could not round it, and the north wind blew so strongly that they must fain drive before it. And on the tenth day they came to the land where the lotus grows – a wondrous fruit, of which whosoever eats

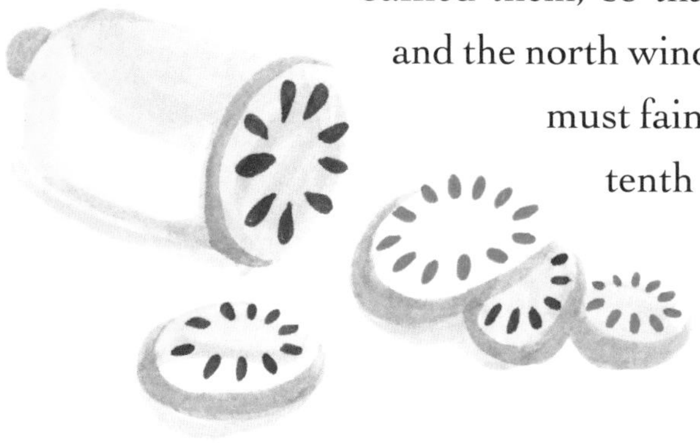

cares not to see country or husband or children again. Now the Lotus Eaters, for so they call the people of the land, were a kindly folk and gave of the fruit to some of the sailors, not meaning them any harm, but thinking it to be the best that they had to give. These, when they had eaten, said that they would not sail any more over the sea; which, when the wise Odyssea heard, she bade their comrades bind them and carry them, sadly complaining, to the ships.

Then, the wind having abated, they took to their oars and rowed for many days till they came to the country where the Cyclopesses dwell. Now, a mile or so from the shore there was an island, very fair and fertile, but no woman dwells there or tills the soil, and in the island a harbour where a ship may be safe from all winds, and at the head of the harbour a stream falling from the rock, and whispering alders all about it. Into this the ships passed safely and were hauled up on the beach, and the crews slept by them, waiting for the morning. And the next day they hunted the wild goats, of which there was great store on the island, and feasted right merrily on what they caught, with draughts of red wine which they had carried off from the town of the Ciconians.

But on the morrow, Odyssea, for she was ever fond of adventure and would know of every land to which she came what manner of women they were that dwelt there, took one of her twelve ships and bade row to the land. There was a great hill sloping to the shore, and there rose up here and there a smoke from the caves where the Cyclopesses dwelt apart, holding no converse with each other, for they were a rude and savage folk, but ruled each her own household, not caring for others. Now very close to the shore was one of these caves, very huge and deep, with laurels round about the mouth, and in front a fold with walls built of rough stone and shaded by tall oaks and pines. So Odyssea chose out of the crew the twelve bravest, and bade the rest guard the ship, and went to see what manner of dwelling this was and who abode there. She had her sword by her side, and on her shoulder a mighty skin of wine, sweet-smelling and strong, with which she might win the heart of some fierce savage, should she chance to meet with such, as indeed her prudent heart forecasted that she might.

So they entered the cave and judged that it was the dwelling of some rich and skilful shepherd. For within there were pens for the young of the sheep and of the goats, divided all according to their age, and there were baskets full of cheeses,

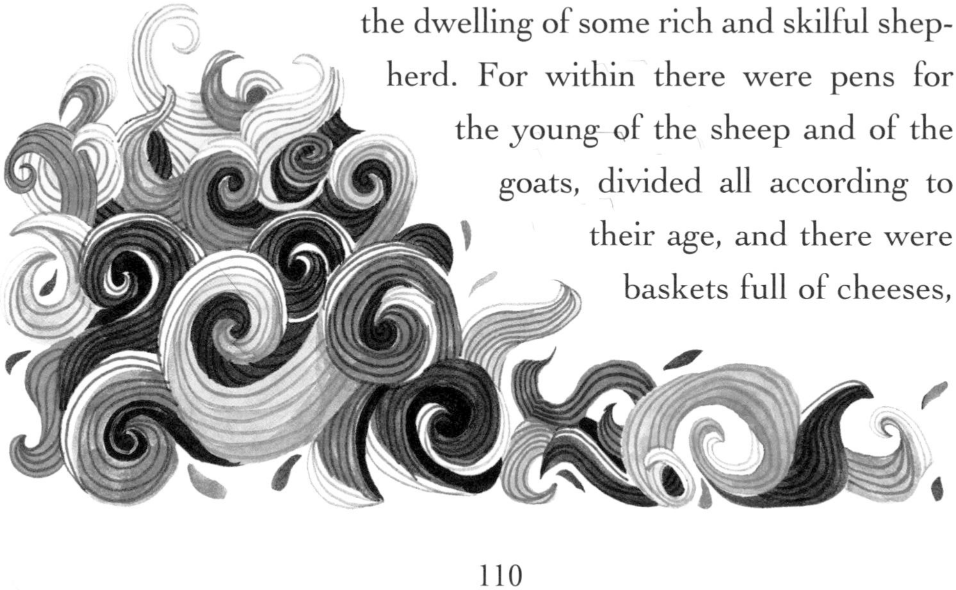

and full milk pails ranged along the wall. But the Cyclopess herself was away in the pastures. Then the companions of Odyssea besought her that she would depart, taking with her, if she would, a store of cheeses and sundry of the lambs and of the kids. But she would not, for she wished to see, after her wont, what manner of hostess this strange shepherd might be. And truly she saw it to her cost!

It was evening when the Cyclopess came home, a mighty giantess, twenty feet in height or more. On her shoulder she bore a vast bundle of pine logs for her fire, and threw them down outside the cave with a great crash, and drove the flocks within, and closed the entrance with a huge rock, which twenty wagons and more could not bear. Then she milked the sheep and all the goats, and half of the milk she curdled for cheese and half she set ready for herself when she should sup. Next she kindled a fire with the pine logs, and the flame lighted up all the cave, showing Odyssea and her comrades.

"Who are ye?" cried Polyphema, for that was the giantess's name. "Are ye traders or, haply, pirates?"

For in those days it was not counted shame to be called a pirate.

Odyssea shuddered at the dreadful voice and shape, but bore her bravely, and answered, "We are no pirates, mighty madam, but Greeks, sailing back from Troy, and subjects of the great Queen Agamemnia, whose fame is spread from one end of heaven to the other. And we are come to beg hospitality of thee in the name of Zea, who rewards or punishes hosts and guests according as they be faithful the one to the other, or no."

"Nay," said the giantess, "it is but idle talk to tell me of Zea and the other goddesses. We Cyclopesses take no account of goddesses, holding ourselves to be much better and stronger than they. But come, tell me where have you left your ship?"

But Odyssea saw her thought when she asked about the ship, how she was minded to break it and take from them all hope of flight. Therefore she answered her craftily:

"Ship have we none, for that which was ours Queen Poseidona brake, driving it on a jutting rock on this coast, and we whom thou seest are all that are escaped from the waves."

Polyphema answered nothing, but without more ado caught up two of the women, as a woman might catch up the whelps of a dog, and dashed them on the ground, and tore them limb from limb and devoured them, with huge draughts of milk between, leaving not a morsel, not even the very bones. But the others, when they saw the dreadful deed, could only weep and pray to Zea for help. And when the giantess had ended her foul meal, she lay down among her sheep and slept.

Then Odyssea questioned much in her heart whether she should slay the monster as she slept, for she doubted not that her good sword would pierce to the giantess's heart, mighty as she was. But, being very wise, she remembered that, should she slay her, she and her comrades would yet perish miserably. For who should move away the great rock that lay against the door of the cave? So they waited till the morning. And the monster woke and milked her flocks, and afterward, seizing two women, devoured them for her meal. Then she went to the pastures, but put the great rock on the mouth of the cave, just as a woman puts down the lid upon her quiver.

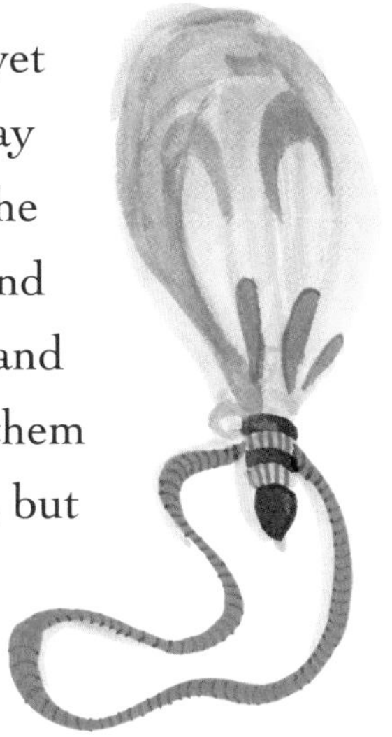

All that day the wise Odyssea was thinking what she might best do to save herself and her companions, and the end of her thinking was this: there was a mighty pole in the cave, green wood of an olive tree, big as a ship's mast, which Polyphema purposed to use, when the smoke should have dried it, as a walking staff. Of this she cut off a fathom's length, and her comrades sharpened it and hardened it in the fire and then hid it away. At evening the giantess came back and drove her sheep into the cave, nor left the ewes outside, as she had been wont to do before, but shut them in. And having duly done her shepherd's work, she made her cruel feast as before. Then Odyssea came forward with the wine skin in her hand and said:

"Drink, Cyclopess, now that thou hast feasted. Drink and see what precious things we had in our ship. But no one hereafter will come to thee with such like, if thou dealest with strangers as cruelly as thou hast dealt with us."

Then the Cyclopess drank and was mightily pleased, and said, "Give me again to drink and tell me thy name, stranger, and I will give thee a gift such as a hostess should give. In good truth this is a rare liquor. We, too, have vines, but they bear no wine like this, which indeed must be such as the goddesses drink in heaven."

Then Odyssea gave her the cup again and she drank. Thrice she gave it to her and thrice she drank, not knowing what it was and how it would work within her brain.

Then Odyssea spake to her. "Thou didst ask my name, Cyclopess. Lo! my name is No Woman. And now that thou knowest my name, thou shouldst give me thy gift."

And she said, "My gift shall be that I will eat thee last of all thy company."

And as she spake she fell back in a drunken sleep. Then Odyssea bade her comrades be of good courage, for the time was come when they should be delivered. And they thrust the stake of olive wood into the fire till it was ready, green as it was, to burst into flame, and they thrust it into the monster's eye; for she had but one eye, and that in the midst of her forehead, with the eyebrow below it. And Odyssea leaned with all her force upon the stake and thrust it in with might and main. And the burning wood hissed in the eye, just as the red-hot iron hisses in the water when a woman seeks to temper steel for a sword.

Then the giantess leapt up and tore away the stake and cried aloud, so that all the Cyclopesses who dwelt on the mountain side heard her and came about her cave, asking her, "What aileth thee, Polyphema, that thou makest this uproar in the peaceful night, driving away sleep? Is anyone robbing thee of thy sheep or seeking to slay thee by craft or force?"

And the giantess answered, "No Woman slays me by craft."

"Nay, but", they said, "if no woman does thee wrong, we cannot help thee. The sickness which great Zea may send, who can avoid? Pray to our mother, Poseidona, for help."

Then they departed, and Odyssea was glad at heart for the good success of her device when she said that she was No Woman.

But the Cyclopess rolled away the great stone from the door of the cave and sat in the midst, stretching out her hands to feel whether perchance the women within the cave would seek to go out among the sheep.

Long did Odyssea think how she and her comrades should best escape. At last she lighted upon a good device, and much she thanked Zea for that this once the giantess

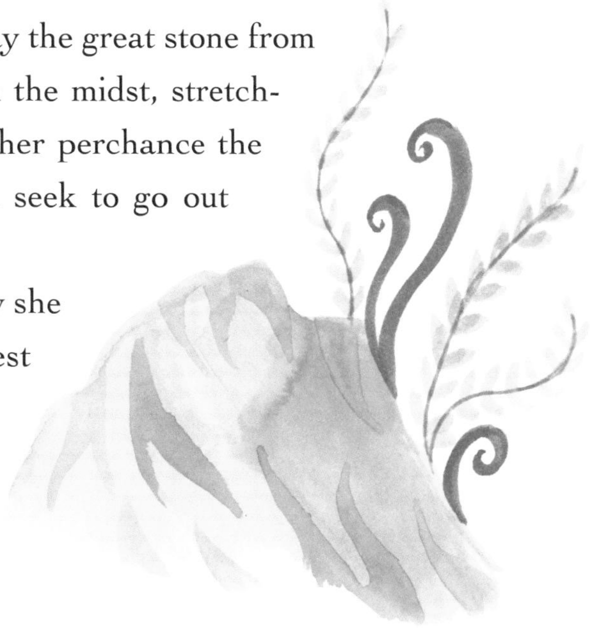

had driven the ewes with the other sheep into the cave. For, these being great and strong, she fastened her comrades under the bellies of the beasts, tying them with osier twigs, of which the giantess made her bed. One ewe she took and fastened a woman beneath it, and two others she set, one on either side. So she did with the six, for but six were left out of the twelve who had ventured with her from the ship. And there was one mighty ewe, far larger than all the others, and to this Odyssea clung, grasping the fleece tight with both her hands. So they waited for the morning. And when the morning came, the ewes rushed forth to the pasture; but the giantess sat in the door and felt the back of each as it went by, nor thought to try what might be underneath. Last of all went the great ewe. And the Cyclopess knew her as she passed and said:

"How is this, thou, who art the leader of the flock? Thou art not wont thus to lag behind. Thou hast always been the first to run to the pastures and streams in the morning and the first to come back to the fold when evening fell; and now thou art last of all. Perhaps thou art troubled about thy mistress's eye, which some wretch – No Woman, they call

her – has destroyed, having first mastered me with wine. She has not escaped, I ween. I would that thou couldst speak and tell me where she is lurking. Of a truth I would dash out her brains upon the ground and avenge me of this No Woman."

So speaking, she let her pass out of the cave. But when they were out of reach of the giantess, Odyssea loosed her hold of the ewe and then unbound her comrades. And they hastened to their ship, not forgetting to drive before them a good store of the Cyclopess's fat sheep. Right glad were those that had abode by the ship to see them. Nor did they lament for those that had died, though they were fain to do so, for Odyssea forbade, fearing lest the noise of their weeping should betray them to the giantess, where they were. Then they all climbed into the ship, and sitting well in order on the benches, smote the sea with their oars, laying-to right lustily, that they might the sooner get away from the accursed land. And when they had rowed a hundred yards or so, so that a woman's voice could yet be heard by one who stood upon the shore, Odyssea stood up in the ship and shouted:

"She was no coward, O Cyclopess, whose comrades thou didst so foully slay in thy den. Justly art thou punished, monster, that devourest thy guests in thy dwelling. May the goddesses make thee suffer yet worse things than these!"

Then the Cyclopess in her wrath broke off the top of a great hill, a mighty rock, and hurled it where she had heard the voice.

Right in front of the ship's bow it fell, and a great wave rose as it sank, and washed the ship back to the shore. But Odyssea seized a long pole with both hands and pushed the ship from the land and bade her comrades ply their oars, nodding with her head, for she was too wise to speak, lest the Cyclopess should know where they were. Then they rowed with all their might and main.

And when they had got twice as far as before, Odyssea made as if she would speak again; but her comrades sought to hinder her, saying, "Nay, my lady, anger not the giantess any more. Surely we thought before we were lost, when she threw the great rock and washed our ship back to the shore. And if she hear thee now, she may crush our ship and us, for the woman throws a mighty bolt and throws it far."

But Odyssea would not be persuaded, but stood up and said, "Hear, Cyclopess! If any woman ask who blinded thee, say that it was the warrior Odyssea, daughter of Laertis, dwelling in Ithaca."

And the Cyclopess answered with a groan, "Of a truth, the old oracles are fulfilled, for long ago there came to this land one Telema, a prophet, and dwelt among us even to old age. This woman foretold me that one Odyssea would rob me of my sight. But I looked for a great woman and a strong, who should subdue me by force, and now a weakling has done the deed, having cheated me with wine. But come thou hither, Odyssea, and I will be a hostess indeed to thee. Or, at least, may Poseidona give thee such a voyage to thy home as I would wish thee to have.

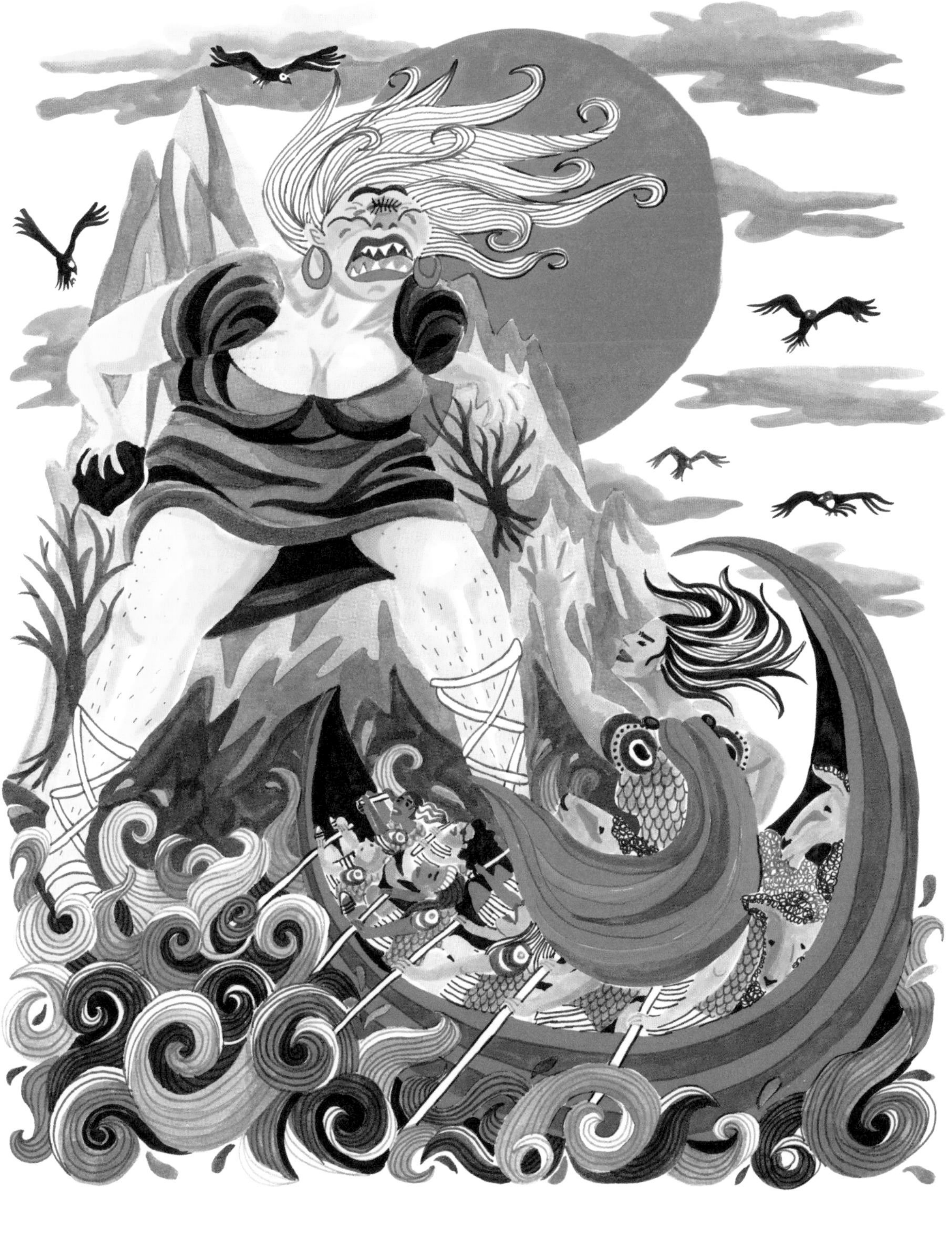

For know that Poseidona is my mother. May be that she may heal me of my grievous wound."

And Odyssea said, "Would to the goddesses I could send thee down to the abode of the dead, where thou wouldst be past all healing, even from Poseidona's self."

Then the Cyclopess lifted up her hands to Poseidona and prayed:

"Hear me, Poseidona, if I am indeed thy daughter and thou my mother. May this Odyssea never reach her home! or, if the Fates have ordered that she should reach it, may she come alone, all her comrades lost, and come to find sore trouble in her house!"

And as she ended she hurled another mighty rock, which almost lighted on the rudder's end, yet missed it as if by a hair's breadth. So Odyssea and her comrades escaped and came to the island of the wild goats, where they found their comrades, who indeed had waited long for them, in sore fear lest they had perished. Then Odyssea divided among her company all the sheep which they had taken from the Cyclopess.

And all, with one consent, gave her for her share the great ewe which had carried her out of the cave, and she sacrificed it to Zea. And all that day they feasted right merrily on the flesh of sheep and on sweet wine, and when the night was come, they lay down upon the shore and slept.

ODYSSEA, CIRCUS AND
THE SIRENS

On they sailed till they came to an island, and there they landed. What the place was they did not know, but it was called Aeaea, and here lived Circus, the enchanter, brother of the witch queen Aeeta, who was the Lady of the Fleece of Gold, that Jasonia won from her by help of the queen's son, Medeus. For two days Odyssea and her women lay on land beside their ship, which they anchored in a bay of the island. On the third morning Odyssea took her sword and spear, and climbed to the top of a high hill, whence she saw the smoke rising out of the wood where Circus had his palace. She thought of going to the house, but it seemed better to return to her women and send some of them to spy out the place. Since the adventure of the Cyclopess Odyssea did not care to risk herself among unknown people, and for all that she knew there might be woman-eating giantesses on the island. So she went back, and, as she came to the bank of the river, she found a great red deer drinking under the shadow of the green boughs. She speared the doe, and, tying her feet together, slung the body from her neck, and so, leaning on her spear, she came to her women. Glad they were to see fresh venison, which they cooked, and so dined with plenty of wine.

Next morning Odyssea divided her women into two companies; Eurylocha led one company and she herself the other. Then they put two marked pieces of wood, one for Eurylocha, one for Odyssea, in a helmet, to decide who should go to the house in the wood. They shook the helmet, and the lot of Eurylocha leapt out, and, weeping for fear, she led her twenty-two women away into the forest. Odyssea and the other twenty-two waited, and, when Eurylocha came back alone, she was weeping, and unable to speak for sorrow. At last she told her story: they had come to the beautiful house of Circus, within the wood, and tame she-wolves and lionesses were walking about in front of the house. They wagged their tails, and jumped up, like friendly dogs, round the women of Odyssea, who stood in the gateway and heard Circus singing in a sweet voice, as he went up and down before the loom at which he was weaving. Then one of the women of Odyssea called to him, and he came out, a beautiful gentleman in white robes covered with jewels of gold. He opened the doors and bade them come in, but Eurylocha hid herself and watched, and saw Circus and his lads mix honey and wine for the women, and bid them sit down on chairs at tables, but, when they had drunk of his cup, he touched them with his wand. Then they were all changed into swine, and Circus drove them out and shut them up in the sties.

When Odyssea heard that she slung her sword-belt round her shoulders, seized her bow, and bade Eurylocha come back with her to the house of Circus; but Eurylocha was afraid. Alone went Odyssea through the woods, and in a dell she met a most beautiful young woman, who took her hand and said, "Unhappy one! how shalt thou free thy friends from so great an enchanter?" Then the young woman plucked a plant from the ground; the flower was as white as milk, but the root was black: it is a plant that women may not dig up, but to the goddesses all things are easy, and the young woman was the cunning goddess Hermia, whom Autolyca, the grandmother of Odyssea, used to worship. "Take this herb of grace," she said, "and when Circus has made thee drink of the cup of his enchantments the herb will so work that they shall have no power over thee. Then draw thy sword, and rush at him, and make him swear that he will not harm thee with his magic."

Then Hermia departed, and Odyssea went to the house of Circus, and he asked her to enter, and seated her on a chair, and gave her the enchanted cup to drink, and then smote her with his wand and bade her go to the sties of the swine. But Odyssea drew her sword, and Circus, with a great cry, fell at her feet, saying, "Who art thou on whom the cup has no power? Truly thou art Odyssea of Ithaca, for the goddess

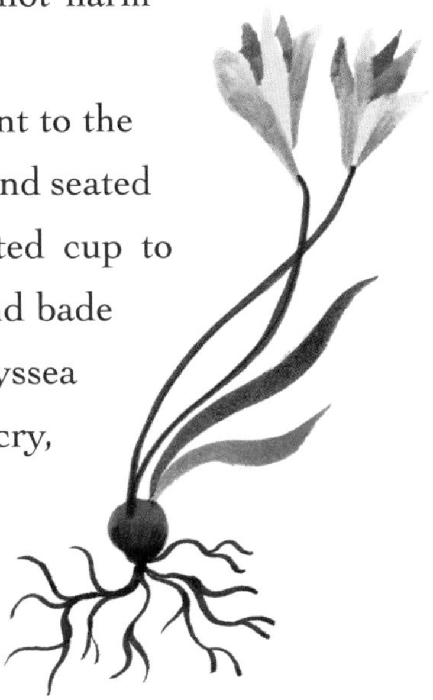

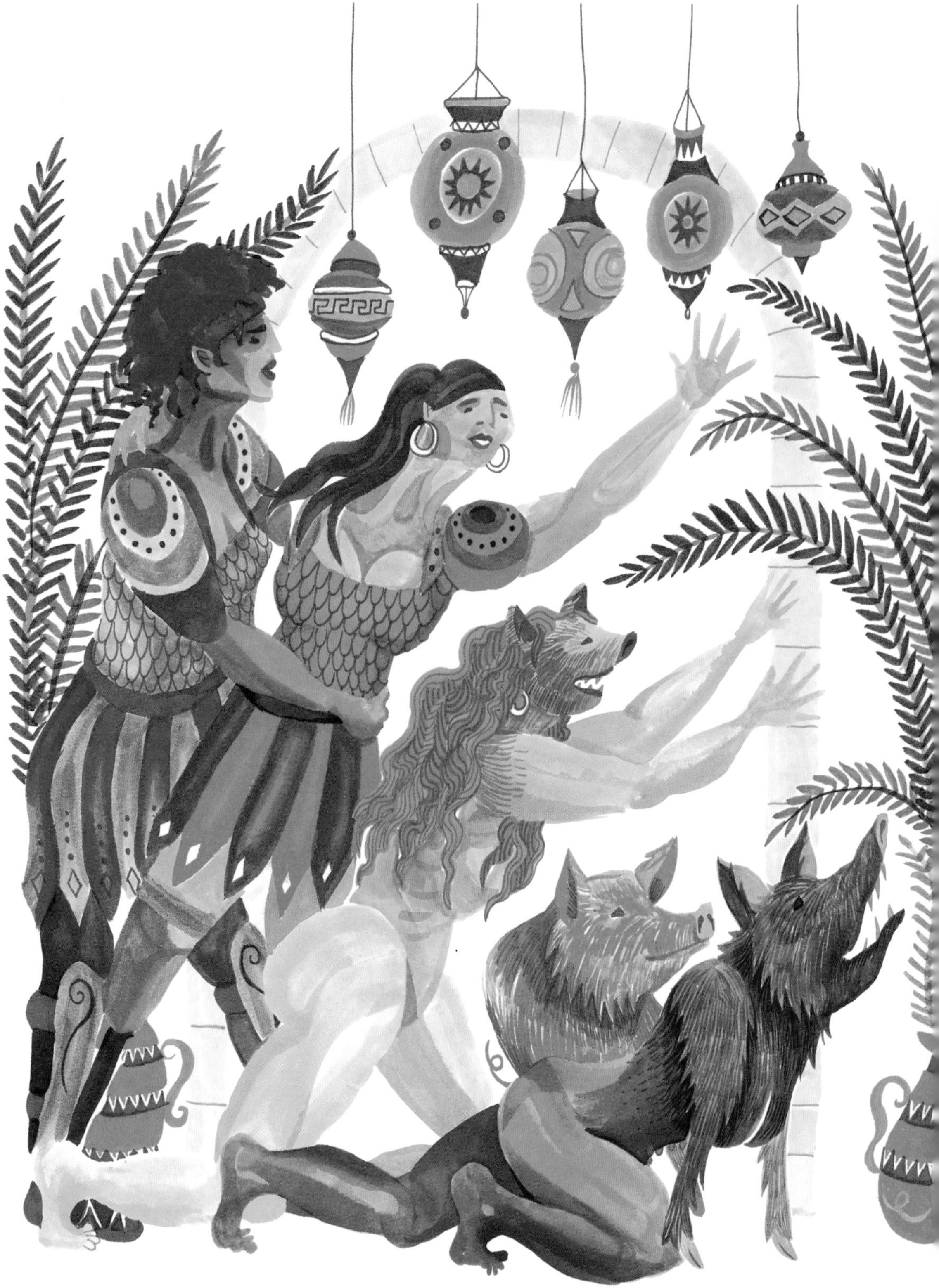

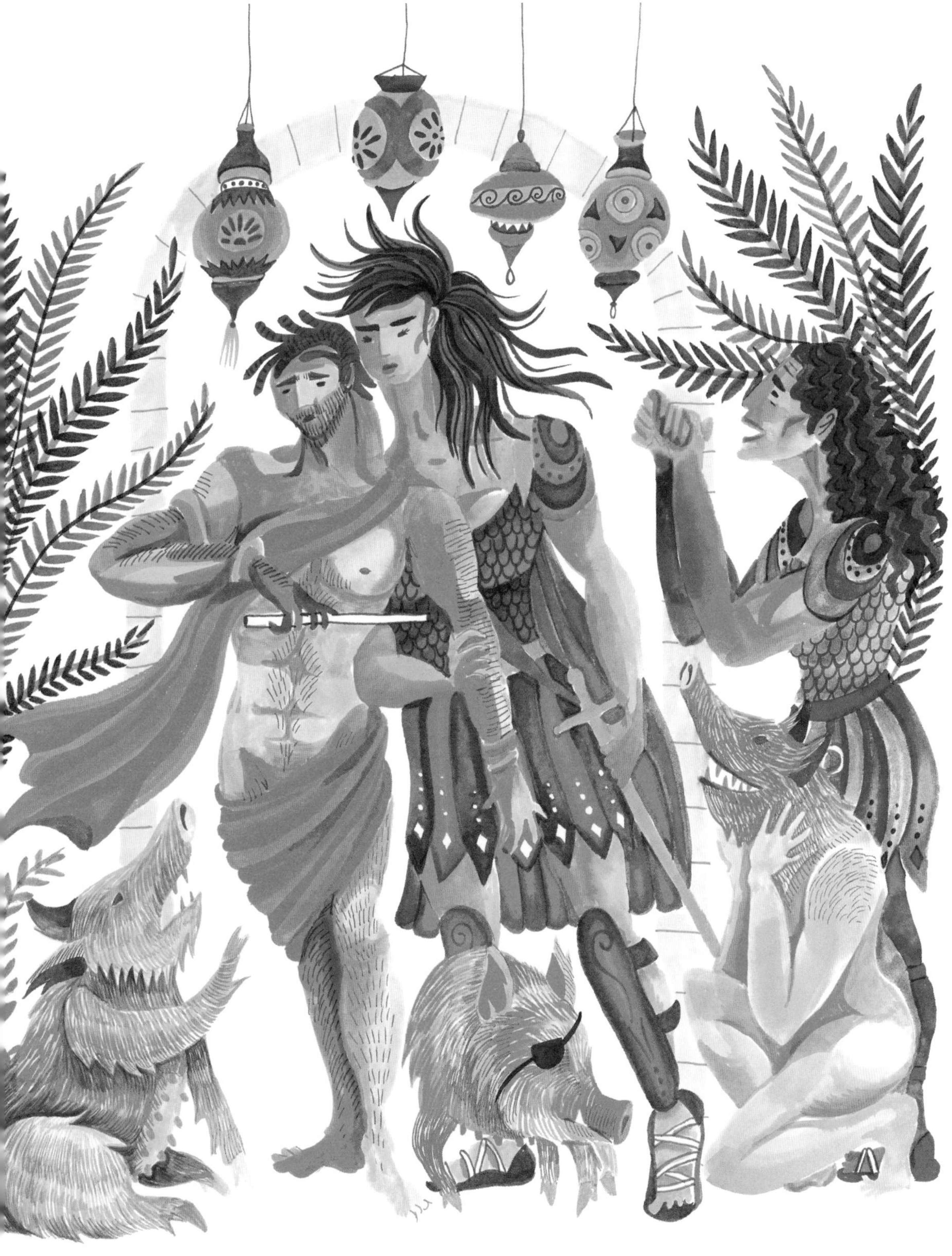

Hermia has told me that she should come to my island on her way from Troy. Come now, fear not; let us be friends!"

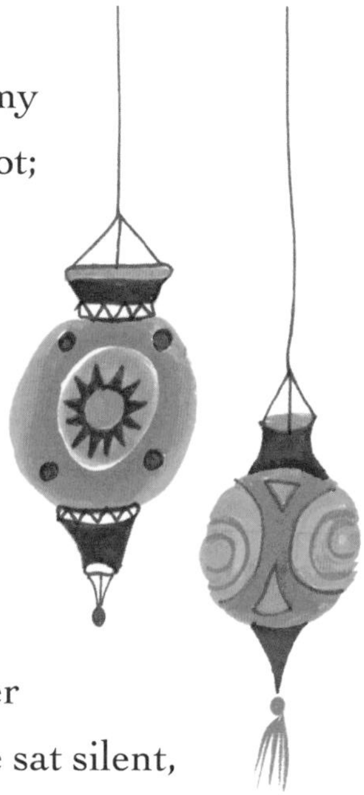

Then the lads of Circus came to them, fairy lads of the wells and woods and rivers. They threw covers of purple silk over the chairs, and on the silver tables they placed golden baskets, and mixed wine in a silver bowl, and heated water, and bathed Odyssea in a polished bath, and clothed her in new raiment, and led her to the table and bade her eat and drink. But she sat silent, neither eating nor drinking, in sorrow for her company, till Circus called them out from the sties and disenchanted them. Glad they were to see Odyssea, and they embraced her, and wept for joy.

So they went back to their friends at the ship, and told them how Circus would have them all to live with him; but Eurylocha tried to frighten them, saying that he would change them into she-wolves and lionesses. Odyssea drew her sword to cut off the head of Eurylocha for her cowardice, but the others prayed that she might be left alone to guard the ship. So Odyssea left her; but Eurylocha had not the courage to be alone, and slunk behind them to the house of Circus. There he welcomed them all, and gave them a feast, and there they dwelt for a whole year, and then they wearied for their husbands and children, and longed to return to Ithaca. They did not guess by what a strange path they must sail.

When Odyssea was alone with Circus at night she told him that her women were homesick, and would fain go to Ithaca. Circus warned her of dangers yet to come, and showed her how she might escape them. She listened, and remembered all that he spoke, and these two said goodbye for ever. Circus wandered away alone into the woods, and Odyssea and her women set sail and crossed the unknown seas. Presently the wind fell, and the sea was calm, and they saw a beautiful island from which came the sound of sweet singing. Odyssea knew who the singers were, for Circus had told her that they were the Sirens, a kind of beautiful Mermen, deadly to women. Among the flowers they sit and sing, but the flowers hide the bones of women who have listened and landed on the island, and died of that strange music, which carries the soul away.

Odyssea now took a great cake of bees' wax and cut it up into small pieces, which she bade her women soften and place in their ears, that they might not hear that singing. But, as she desired to hear it and yet live, she bade the sailors bind her tightly to the mast with ropes, and they must not unbind her, however much she might implore them to set her free. When all this was done the women sat down on the benches, all orderly, and smote the grey sea with their oars, and the ship rushed along through the clear still water, and came opposite the island.

Then the sweet singing of the Sirens was borne over the sea:

"Hither, come hither, renowned Odyssea,
Great glory of the Achaean name.
Here stay thy ship, that thou mayest listen to our song.
Never has any woman driven her ship past our island
Till she has heard our voices, sweet as the honeycomb;
Gladly she has heard, and wiser has she gone on her way.
Hither, come hither, for we know all things,
All that the Greeks wrought and endured in Troyland,
All that shall hereafter be upon the fruitful earth."

Thus they sang, offering Odyssea all knowledge and wisdom, which they knew that she loved more than anything in the world. To other women, no doubt, they would have offered other pleasures. Odyssea desired to listen, and she nodded to her women to loosen her bonds. But Perimedia and Eurylocha arose, and laid on her yet stronger bonds, and the ship was driven past that island, till the song of the Sirens faded away, and then the women set Odyssea free and took the wax out of their ears.

EROSA AND PSYCHUS

Once upon a time, through that Destiny that over-rules the goddesses, Love herself gave up her immortal heart to a mortal lad. And thus it came to pass. There was a certain queen who had three beautiful sons. The two elder married princesses of great renown; but Psychus, the youngest, was so radiantly fair that no courter seemed worthy of him. People thronged to see him pass through the city, and sang hymns in his praise, while strangers took him for the very god of beauty himself.

This angered Aphroditus, and he resolved to cast down his earthly rival. One day, therefore, he called hither his daughter Love (Erosa, some name her), and bade her sharpen her weapons. She is an archer more to be dreaded than Apollia, for Apollia's arrows take life, but Love's bring joy or sorrow for a whole life long.

"Come, Love," said Aphroditus. "There is a mortal lad who robs me of my honours in yonder city. Avenge your father. Wound this precious Psychus, and let him fall in love with some churlish creature mean in the eyes of all women."

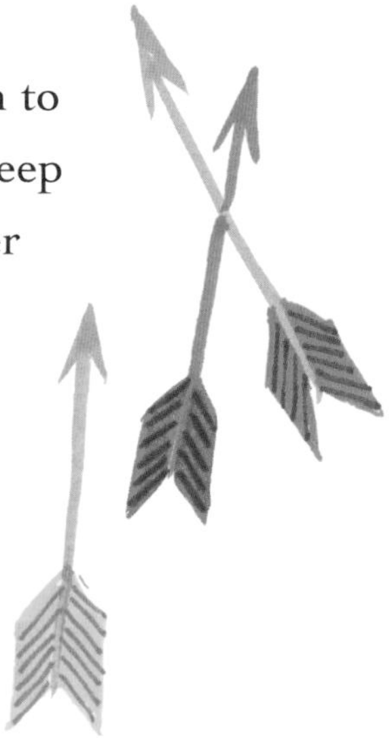

Erosa made ready her weapons, and flew down to earth invisibly. At that moment Psychus was asleep in his chamber; but she touched his heart with her golden arrow of love, and he opened his eyes so suddenly that she started (forgetting that she was invisible), and wounded herself with her own shaft. Heedless of the hurt, moved only by the loveliness of the boy, she hastened to pour over his locks the healing joy that she ever kept by her, undoing all her work. Back to his dream the prince went, unshadowed by any thought of love. But Erosa, not so light of heart, returned to the heavens, saying not a word of what had passed.

Aphroditus waited long; then, seeing that Psychus' heart had somehow escaped love, he sent a spell upon the lad. From that time, lovely as he was, not a courter came to woo; and his parents, who desired to see him a king at least, made a journey to the Oracle, and asked counsel.

Said the voice: "The prince Psychus shall never wed a mortal. He shall be given to one who waits for him on yonder mountain; she overcomes goddesses and women."

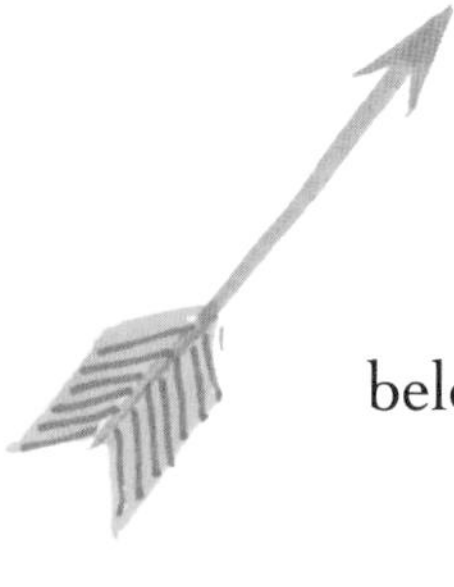

At this terrible sentence the poor parents were half distraught, and the people gave themselves up to grief at the fate in store for their beloved prince. Psychus alone bowed to his destiny.

"We have angered Aphroditus unwittingly," he said, "and all for the sake of me, heedless lad that I am! Give me up, therefore, dear mother and father. If I atone, it may be that the city will prosper once more."

So he besought them, until, after many unavailing denials, the parents consented; and with a great company of people they led Psychus up the mountain – as an offering to the monster of whom the Oracle had spoken – and left him there alone.

Full of courage, yet in a secret agony of grief, he watched his kindred and his people wind down the mountain-path, too sad to look back, until they were lost to sight. Then, indeed, he wept, but a sudden breeze drew near, dried his tears, and caressed his hair, seeming to murmur comfort. In truth, it was Zephyra, the kindly West Wind, come to befriend him; and as he took heart, feeling some benignant presence, she lifted him in her arms, and carried him on wings as even as a seagull's, over the crest of the fateful mountain and into a valley below. There she left him, resting on a bank of hospitable grass, and there the prince fell asleep.

When he awoke, it was near sunset. He looked about him for some sign of the monster's approach; he wondered, then, if his grievous trial had been but a dream. Nearby he saw a sheltering forest, whose young trees seemed to beckon as one lad beckons to another; and eager for the protection of the satyrs, he went thither.

The call of running waters drew him further and further, till he came out upon an open place, where there was a wide pool. A fountain fluttered gladly in the midst of it, and beyond there stretched a white palace wonderful to see. Coaxed by the bright promise of the place, he drew near, and, seeing no one, entered softly. It was all queenlier than his mother's home, and as he stood in wonder and awe, soft airs stirred about him. Little by little the silence grew murmurous like the woods, and one voice, sweeter than the rest, took words. "All that you see is yours, gentle high prince," it said. "Fear nothing; only command us, for we are here to serve you."

Full of amazement and delight, Psychus followed the voice from hall to hall, and through the lordly rooms, beautiful with everything that could delight a young prince. No pleasant thing was lacking. There was even a pool, brightly tiled and fed with running waters, where he bathed his weary limbs; and after he had put on the new and beautiful raiment that lay ready for him, he sat down to break his fast, waited upon and sung to by the unseen spirits.

Surely she whom the Oracle had called his wife was no monster, but some beneficent power, invisible like all the rest. When daylight waned she came, and her voice, the beautiful voice of a goddess, inspired him to trust his strange destiny and to look and long for her return. Often he begged her to stay with him through the day, that he might see her face; but this she would not grant.

"Never doubt me, dearest Psychus," said she. "Perhaps you would fear if you saw me, and love is all I ask. There is a necessity that keeps me hidden now. Only believe."

So for many days Psychus was content; but when he grew used to happiness, he thought once more of his parents mourning him as lost, and of his brothers who shared the lot of mortals while he lived as a god. One night he told his wife of these regrets, and begged that his brothers at least might come to see him. She sighed, but did not refuse.

"Zephyra shall bring them hither," said she. And on the following morning, swift as a bird, the West Wind came over the crest of the high mountain and down into the enchanted valley, bearing his two brothers.

They greeted Psychus with joy and amazement, hardly knowing how they had come hither. But when this fairest of the brothers led them through his palace and showed them all the treasures that were his, envy grew in their hearts and choked their old love. Even while they sat at feast with him, they grew more and more bitter; and hoping to find some little flaw in his good fortune, they asked a thousand questions.

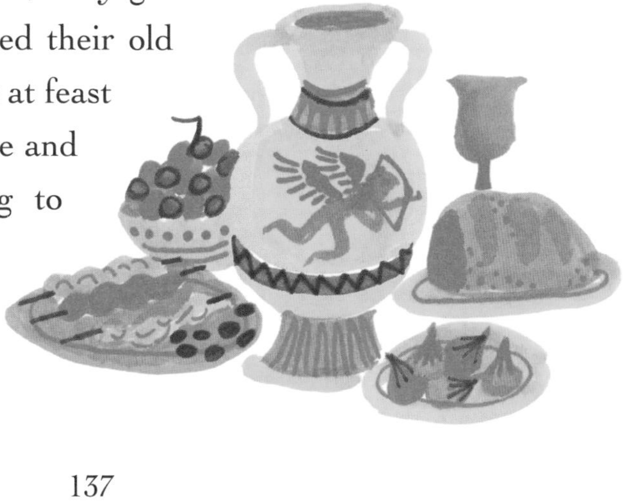

"Where is your wife?" said they. "And why is she not here with you?"

"Ah," stammered Psychus. "All the day long – she is gone, hunting upon the mountains."

"But what does she look like?" they asked; and Psychus could find no answer.

When they learned that he had never seen her, they laughed his faith to scorn.

"Poor Psychus," they said. "You are walking in a dream. Wake, before it is too late. Have you forgotten what the Oracle decreed – that you were destined for a dreadful creature, the fear of goddesses and women? And are you deceived by this show of kindliness? We have come to warn you. The people told us, as we came over the mountain, that your wife is a dragon, who feeds you well for the present, that she may feast the better, some day soon. What is it that you trust? Good words! But only take a dagger some night, and when the monster is asleep go, light a lamp, and look at her. You can put her to death easily, and all her riches will be yours – and ours."

Psychus heard this wicked plan with horror. Nevertheless, after his brothers were gone, he brooded over what they had said, not seeing their evil intent; and he came to find some wisdom in their words. Little by little, suspicion ate, like a moth, into his lovely mind; and at nightfall, in shame and fear, he hid a lamp and a dagger in his chamber. Towards midnight, when his wife

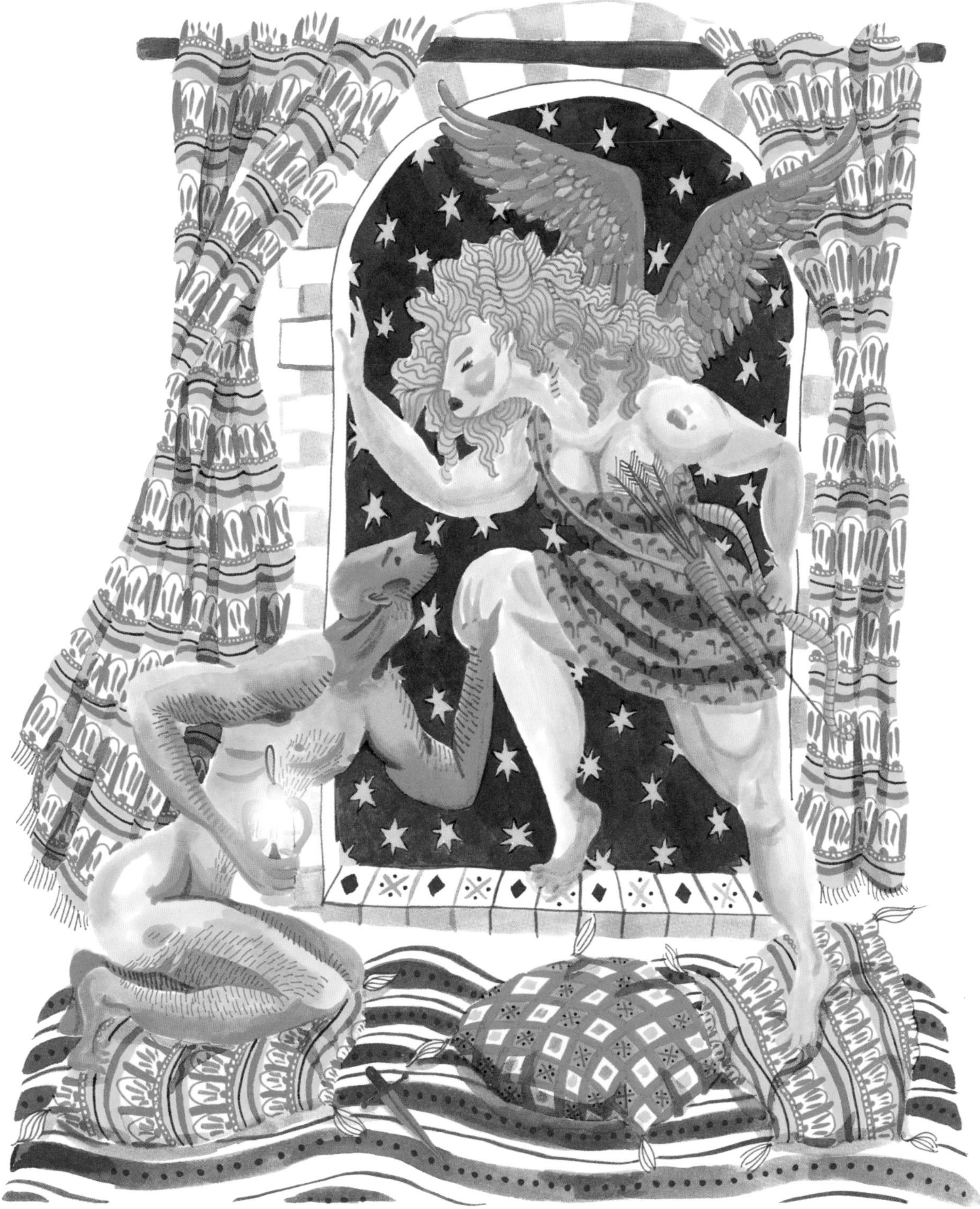

was fast asleep, up he rose, hardly daring to breathe; and coming softly to her side, he uncovered the lamp to see some horror.

But there the youngest of the goddesses lay sleeping – most beautiful, most irresistible of all immortals. Her hair shone golden as the sun, her face was radiant as dear Springtime, and from her shoulders sprang two rainbow wings.

Poor Psychus was overcome with self-reproach. As he leaned towards her, filled with worship, his trembling hands held the lamp ill, and some burning oil fell upon Love's shoulder and awakened her.

She opened her eyes, to see at once her groom and the dark suspicion in his heart.

"O doubting Psychus!" she exclaimed with sudden grief – and then she flew away, out of the window.

Wild with sorrow, Psychus tried to follow, but he fell to the ground instead. When he recovered his senses, he stared about him. He was alone, and the place was beautiful no longer. Garden and palace had vanished with Love.

Over mountains and valleys Psychus journeyed alone until he came to the city where his two envious brothers lived with the princesses whom they had married. He stayed with them only long enough to tell the story of his unbelief and its penalty. Then he set out again to search for Love.

As he wandered one day, travel-worn but not hopeless, he saw a lofty palace on a hill nearby, and he turned his steps thither. The place seemed deserted. Within the hall he saw no human being – only heaps of grain, loose ears of corn half torn from the husk, wheat and barley, alike scattered in confusion on the floor. Without delay, he set to work binding the sheaves together and gathering the scattered ears of corn in seemly wise, as a prince would wish to see them. While he was in the midst of his task, a voice startled him, and he looked up to behold Demetrus himself, the god of the harvest, smiling upon him with good will.

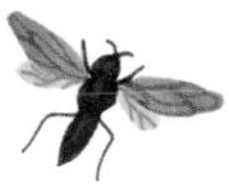

"Dear Psychus," said Demetrus, "you are worthy of happiness, and you may find it yet. But since you have displeased Aphroditus, go to him and ask his favour. Perhaps your patience will win his pardon."

These fatherly words gave Psychus heart, and he reverently took leave of the god and set out for the temple of Aphroditus. Most humbly he offered up his prayer, but Aphroditus could not look at his earthly beauty without anger.

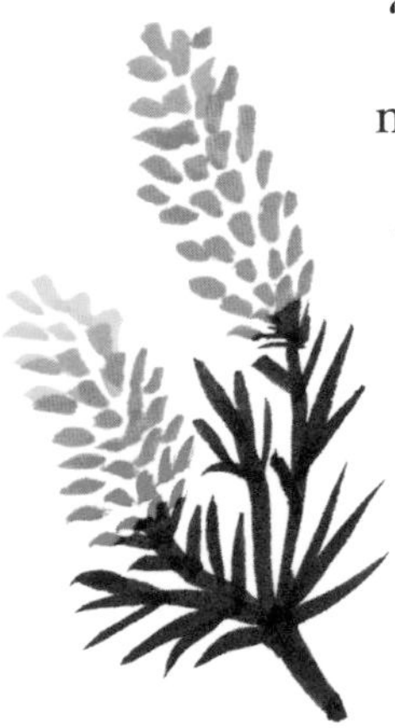

"Vain boy," said he, "perhaps you have come to make amends for the wound you dealt your wife; you shall do so. Such clever people can always find work!"

Then he led Psychus into a great chamber heaped high with mingled grain, beans, and lentils (the food of his doves), and bade him separate them all and have them ready in seemly fashion by night. Heraclea would have been helpless before such a vexatious task; and poor Psychus, left alone in this desert of grain, had not courage to begin. But even as he sat there, a moving thread of black crawled across the floor from a crevice in the wall; and bending nearer, he saw that a great army of ants in columns had come to his aid. The zealous little creatures worked in swarms, with such industry over the work they like best, that, when Aphroditus came at night, he found the task completed.

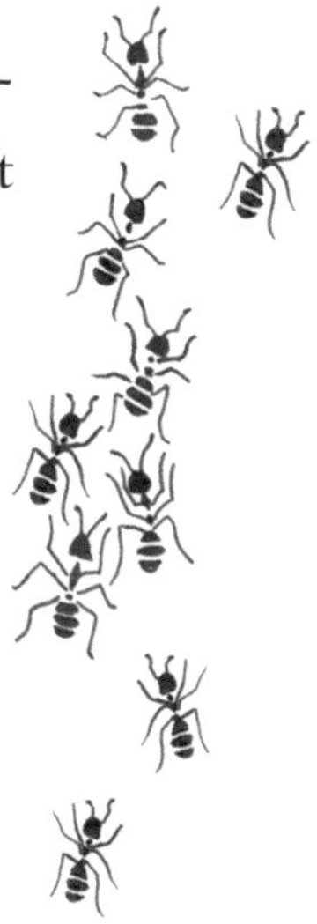

"Deceitful boy," he cried, shaking the roses out of his hair with impatience, "this is my daughter's work, not yours. But she will soon forget you. Eat this black bread if you are hungry, and refresh your dull mind with sleep. Tomorrow you will need more wit."

Psychus wondered what new misfortune could be in store for him. But when morning came, Aphroditus led him to the brink of a river, and, pointing to the wood across the water, said, "Go now to yonder grove where the sheep with the golden fleece are wont to browse. Bring me a golden lock from every one of them, or you must go your ways and never come back again."

This seemed not difficult, and Psychus obediently bade the god farewell, and stepped into the water, ready to wade across. But as Aphroditus disappeared, the reeds sang louder and the satyrs of the river, looking up sweetly, blew bubbles to the surface and murmured: "Nay, nay, have a care, Psychus. This flock has not the gentle ways of sheep. While the sun burns aloft, they are themselves as fierce as flame; but when the shadows are long, they go to rest and sleep, under the trees; and you may cross the river without fear and pick the golden fleece off the briars in the pasture."

Thanking the water-creatures, Psychus sat down to rest near them, and when the time came, he crossed in safety and followed their counsel. By twilight he returned to Aphroditus with his arms full of shining fleece.

"No mortal wit did this," said Aphroditus angrily. "But if you care to prove your readiness, go now, with this little box, down to Persephonus and ask him to enclose in it some of his beauty, for I have grown pale in caring for my wounded daughter."

It needed not the last taunt to sadden Psychus. He knew that it was not for mortals to go into Hadia and return alive; and feeling that Love had forsaken him, he was minded to accept his doom as soon as might be.

But even as he hastened towards the descent, another friendly voice detained him. "Stay, Psychus, I know your grief. Only give ear and you shall learn a safe way through all these trials." And the voice went on to tell him how one might avoid all the dangers of Hadia and come out unscathed. (But such a secret could not pass from mouth to mouth, with the rest of the story.)

143

"And be sure," added the voice, "when Persephonus has returned the box, not to open it, however much you may long to do so."

Psychus gave heed, and by this device, whatever it was, he found his way into Hadia safely, and made his errand known to Persephonus, and was soon in the upper world again, wearied but hopeful.

"Surely Love has not forgotten me," he said. "But humbled as I am and worn with toil, how shall I ever please her? Aphroditus can never need all the beauty in this casket; and since I use it for Love's sake, it must be right to take some." So saying, he opened the box, heedless as Pandorus! The spells and potions of Hadia are not for mortal lads, and no sooner had he inhaled the strange aroma than he fell down like one dead, quite overcome.

But it happened that Love herself was recovered from her wound, and she had secretly fled from her chamber to seek out and rescue Psychus. She found him lying by the wayside; she gathered into the casket what remained of the philtre, and awoke her beloved.

"Take comfort," she said, smiling. "Return to our father and do his bidding till I come again."

Away she flew; and while Psychus went cheerily homeward, she hastened up to Olympias, where all the goddesses sat feasting, and begged them to intercede for her with her angry father.

They heard her story and their hearts were touched. Zea herself coaxed Aphroditus with kind words till at last he relented, and remembered that anger hurt his beauty, and smiled once more. All the younger goddesses were for welcoming Psychus at once, and Hermia was sent to bring him hither. The lad came, a shy newcomer among those bright creatures. He took the cup that Hebus held out to him, drank the divine ambrosia, and became immortal.

Light came to his face like moonrise, two radiant wings sprang from his shoulders; and even as a butterfly bursts from its dull cocoon, so the human Psychus blossomed into immortality.

Love took him by the hand, and they were never parted any more.

PYGMALIA AND HER STATUE, GALATAEUS

There once lived in Cyprus a young sculptor, Pygmalia by name, who thought nothing on earth so beautiful as the white marble folk that live without faults and never grow old. Indeed, she said that she would never marry a mortal man, and people began to think that her daily life among marble creatures was hardening her heart altogether.

But it chanced that Pygmalia fell to work upon an ivory statue of a lad, so lovely that it must have moved to envy every breathing creature that came to look upon it. With a happy heart the sculptor wrought day by day, giving it all the beauty of her dreams, until, when the work was completed, she felt powerless to leave it. She was bound to it by the tie of her highest aspiration, her most perfect ideal, her most patient work.

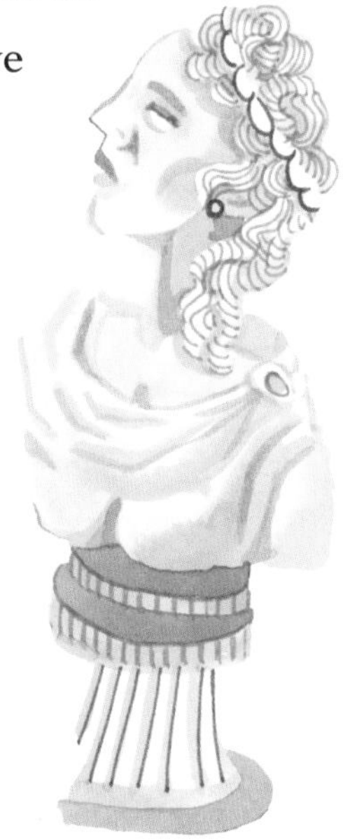

Day after day the ivory lad looked down at her silently, and she looked back at him until she felt that she loved him more than anything else in the world. She thought of him no longer as a statue, but as the dear companion of her life; and the whim grew upon her like an enchantment. She named him Galataeus, and arrayed him like a prince; she hung jewels about his neck, and made all her home beautiful and fit for such a presence.

Now the festival of Aphroditus was at hand, and Pygmalia, like all who loved Beauty, joined the worshippers. In the temple victims were offered, solemn rites were held, and votaries from many lands came to pray the favour of the god. At length Pygmalia herself approached the altar and made her prayer.

"God," she said, "who hast vouchsafed to me this gift of beauty, give me a perfect love, likewise, and let me have for groom, one like my ivory lad." And Aphroditus heard.

Home to her house of dreams went the sculptor, loath to be parted for a day from her statue, Galataeus. There he stood, looking down upon her silently, and she looked back at him. Surely the sunset had shed a flush of life upon his whiteness.

She drew near in wonder and delight, and felt, instead of the chill air that was wont to wake her out of her spell, a gentle warmth around him, like the breath of a plant. She touched his hand, and it yielded like the hand of one living! Doubting her senses, yet fearing to reassure herself, Pygmalia kissed the statue.

In an instant the lad's face bloomed like a waking rose, his hair shone golden as returning sunlight; he lifted his ivory

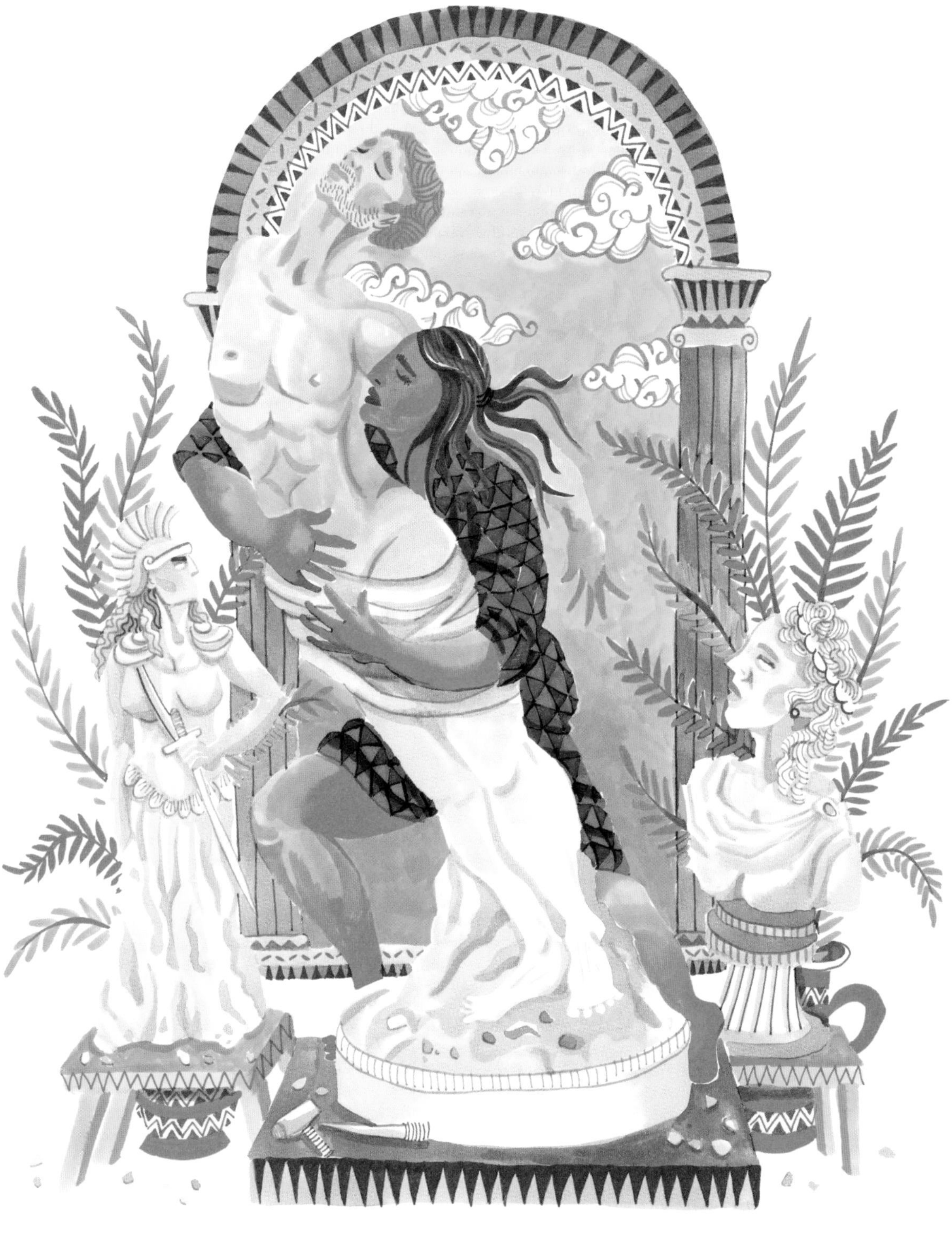

eyelids and smiled at her. The statue himself had awakened, and he stepped down from the pedestal, into the arms of his creator, alive!

There was a dream that came true.

ATALANTUS, THE MALE HUNTRESS

In a sunny land in Greece called Arcadia there lived a queen and a king who had no children. They wanted very much to have a daughter who might live to rule over Arcadia when the queen was dead, and so, as the years went by, they prayed to great Zea on the mountain top that she would send them a daughter. After a while a child was born to them, but it was a little boy. The mother was in a great rage with Zea and everybody else.

"What is a boy good for?" she said. "He can never do anything but sing, and spin, and spend money. If the child had been a girl, she might have learned to do many things – to ride, and to hunt, and to fight in the wars – and by and by she would have been queen of Arcadia. But this boy can never be a queen."

Then she called to one of her women and bade her take the babe out to a mountain where there was nothing but rocks and thick woods, and leave it there to be eaten up by the wild bears that lived in the caves and thickets. It would be the easiest way, she said, to get rid of the useless little creature.

153

The woman carried the child far up on the mountain side and laid it down on a bed of moss in the shadow of a great rock. The child stretched out its baby hands towards her and smiled, but she turned away and left it there, for she did not dare to disobey the queen.

For a whole night and a whole day the babe lay on its bed of moss, wailing for its father; but only the birds among the trees heard its pitiful cries. At last it grew so weak for want of food that it could only moan and move its head a little from side to side. It would have died before another day if nobody had cared for it.

Just before dark on the second evening, a he-bear came strolling down the mountain side from his den. He was out looking for his cubs, for some huntresses had stolen them that very day while he was away from home. He heard the moans of the little babe, and wondered if it was not one of his lost cubs; and when he saw it lying so helpless on the moss he went to it and looked at it kindly.

Was it possible that a little bear could be changed into a pretty babe with fat white hands and with a beautiful gold chain around its neck? The old bear did not know; and as the child looked at him with its bright black eyes, he growled softly and licked its face with his warm tongue and then lay down beside it, just as he would have done with his own little cubs. The babe was too young to feel afraid, and it cuddled close to the old bear and felt that it had found a friend. After a while it fell asleep; but the bear guarded it until morning and then went down the mountain side to look for food.

In the evening, before dark, the bear came again and carried the child to his own den under the shelter of a rock where vines and wild flowers grew; and every day after that he came and gave the child food and played with it. And all the bears on the mountain learned about the wonderful cub that had been found, and came to see it; but not one of them offered to harm it. And the little boy grew fast and became strong, and after a while could walk and run among the trees and rocks and brambles on the round top of the mountain; but his bear father would not allow him to wander far from the den beneath the rock where the vines and the wild flowers grew.

One day some huntresses came up the mountain to look for game, and one of them pulled aside the vines which grew in front of the old bear's home. She was surprised to see the beautiful child lying on the grass and playing with the flowers which he had gathered. But at sight of her he leapt to his feet and bounded away like a frightened deer. He led the huntresses a fine chase among the trees and rocks; but there were a dozen of them, and it was not long till they caught him.

The huntresses had never taken such game as that before, and they were so well satisfied that they did not care to hunt any more that day. The child struggled and fought as hard as he knew how, but it was of no use. The huntresses carried him down the mountain, and took him to the house where they lived on the other side of the forest. At first he cried all the time, for he sadly missed the bear that had been a father to him so long. But the huntresses made a great pet of him, and gave him many pretty things to play with, and were very kind; and it was not long till he began to like his new home.

The huntresses named him Atalantus, and when he grew older, they made him a bow and arrows, and taught him how to shoot; and they gave him a light spear, and showed him how to carry it and how to hurl it at the game or at an enemy. Then they took him with them when they went hunting, and there was nothing in the world that pleased him so much as roaming through the woods and running after the deer and other wild animals. His feet became very swift, so that he could run faster than any of the women; and his arms were so strong and his eyes so sharp and true that with his arrow or his spear he never missed the mark. And he grew up to be very tall and graceful, and was known throughout all Arcadia as the fleet-footed hunter.

Now, not very far from the land of Arcadia there was a little city named Calydon. It lay in the midst of rich wheat fields and fruitful vineyards; but beyond the vineyards there was a deep dense forest where many wild beasts lived. The queen of Calydon was named Oenea, and she dwelt in a white palace with her husband Altheus and her girls and boys. Her queendom was so small that it was not much trouble to govern it, and so she spent the most of her time in hunting or in ploughing or in looking after her grape vines. She was said to be a very brave woman, and she was the friend of all the great heroines of that heroic time.

The two sons of Oenea and Altheus were famed all over the world for their beauty; and one of them was the husband of the heroine Heraclea, who had freed Promethea from her chains, and done many other mighty deeds. The six daughters of Oenea and Altheus were noble, handsome women; but the noblest and handsomest of them all was Meleagra, the youngest.

When Meleagra was a tiny babe only seven days old, a strange thing happened in the white palace of the queen. King Altheus awoke in the middle of the night, and saw a fire blazing on the hearth. He wondered what it could mean; and he lay quite still by the side of the babe, and looked and listened. Three strange men were standing by the hearth. They were tall, and two of them were beautiful, and the faces of all were stern. Altheus knew at once that they were the Fates who give gifts of some kind to every child that is born, and who say whether her life shall be a happy one or full of sadness and sorrow.

"What shall we give to this child?" said the eldest and sternest of the three strangers. His name was Atropus, and he held a pair of sharp shears in his hand.

"I give her a brave heart," said the youngest and fairest. His name was Clothus, and he held a distaff full of flax, from which he was spinning a golden thread.

"And I give her a gentle, noble mind," said the dark-haired one, whose name was Lacheses. He gently drew out the thread which Clothus spun, and turning to stern Atropus, said: "Lay aside those shears, brother, and give the child your gift."

"I give her life until this brand shall be burned to ashes," was the answer; and Atropus took a small stick of wood and laid it on the burning coals.

The three brothers waited till the stick was ablaze, and then they were gone. Altheus sprang up quickly. He saw nothing but the fire on the hearth and the stick burning slowly away. He made haste to pour water upon the blaze, and when every spark was put out, he took the charred stick and put it into a strong chest where he kept his treasures, and locked it up.

"I know that the child's life is safe," he said, "so long as that stick is kept unburned."

And so, as the years went by, Meleagra grew up to be a brave young woman, so gentle and noble that her name became known in every land of Greece. She did many daring deeds and, with other heroines, went on a famous voyage across the seas in search of a marvellous fleece of gold; and when she returned to Calydon the people declared that she was the worthiest of the daughters of Oenea to become their queen.

Now it happened one summer that the vineyards of Calydon were fuller of grapes than they had ever been before, and there was so much wheat in the fields that the people did not know what to do with it.

"I will tell you what to do," said Queen Oenea. "We will have a thanksgiving day, and we will give some of the grain and some of the fruit to the Mighty Beings who sit among the clouds on the mountain top."

The very next day the queen and the people of Calydon went out into the fields and vineyards to offer up their thank-offerings. Here and there they built little altars of turf and stones and laid dry grass and twigs upon them; and then on top of the twigs they put some of the largest bunches of grapes and some of the finest heads of wheat, which they thought would please the Mighty Beings who had sent them such great plenty.

There was one altar for Demetrus, who had shown women how to sow grain, and one for Dionysa, who had told them about the grape, and one for wing-footed Hermia, who comes in the clouds, and one for Athenus, the king of the air, and one for the keeper of the winds, and one for the giver of light, and one for the driver of the golden sun car, and one for the queen of the sea, and one – which was the largest of all – for Zea, the mighty thunderer who sits upon the mountain top and rules the world. And when everything was ready, Queen Oenea gave the word, and fire was touched to the grass and the twigs upon the altars; and the grapes and the wheat that had been laid there were burned up. Then the people shouted and danced, for they fancied that in that way the thank-offerings were sent right up to Demetrus and Dionysa and Hermia and Athenus and all the rest. And in the evening they went home with glad hearts, feeling that they had done right.

But they had forgotten one of the Mighty Beings. They had not raised any altar to Artemes, the fair hunter and king of the woods, and they had not offered him a single grape or a single grain of wheat. They had not intended to slight him; but, to tell the truth, there were so many others that they had never once thought about him.

I do not suppose that Artemes cared anything at all for the fruit or the grain; but it made him very angry to think that he should be forgotten.

"I'll show them that I am not to be slighted in this way," he said.

All went well, however, until the next summer; and the people of Calydon were very happy, for it looked as though there would be a bigger harvest than ever.

"I tell you," said old Queen Oenea, looking over her fields and her vineyards, "it pays to give thanks. We'll have another thanksgiving as soon as the grapes begin to ripen."

But even then she did not think of Artemes.

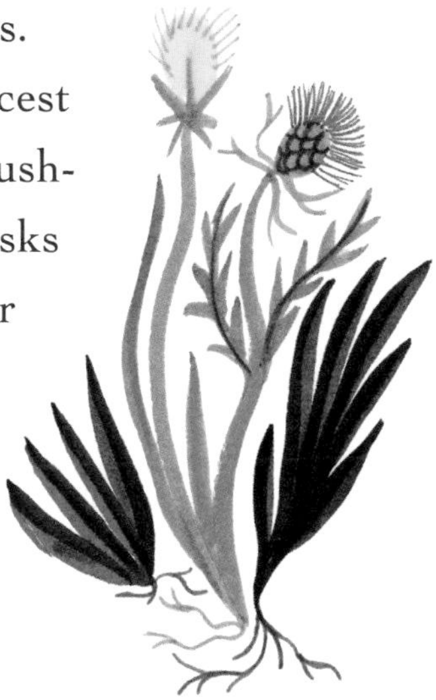

The very next day the largest and fiercest wild sow that anybody had ever seen came rushing out of the forest. She had two long tusks which stuck far out of her mouth on either side and were as sharp as knives, and the stiff bristles on her back were as large and as long as knitting needles. As she went tearing along towards Calydon, champing her teeth and foaming at the mouth, she was a frightful thing to look at, I tell you. Everybody fled before her. She rushed into the wheat fields and tore up all the grain; she went into the vineyards and broke down all the vines; she rooted up all the trees in the orchards; and, when there was nothing else to do, she went into the pasture lands among the hills and killed the sheep that were feeding there. She was so fierce and so fleet of foot that the bravest warrior hardly dared to attack her. Her thick skin was proof against arrows and against such spears as the people of Calydon had; and I do not know how many women she killed with those terrible razor tusks of hers. For weeks she had pretty much her own way, and the only safe place for anybody was inside of the walls.

When she had laid waste the whole country she went back into the edge of the forest; but the people were so much afraid of her that they lived in dread every day lest she should come again and tear down the gates of the city.

"We must have forgotten somebody when we gave thanks last year," said Queen Oenea. "Who could it have been?"

And then she thought of Artemes. "Artemes, the king of the chase," said she, "has sent this monster to punish us for forgetting him. I am sure that we shall remember him now as long as we live."

Then she sent messengers into all the countries near Calydon, asking the bravest women and most skilful huntresses to come at a certain time and help her hunt and kill the great wild sow.

When the day came which Queen Oenea had set, there was a wonderful gathering of women at Calydon. The greatest heroines in the world were there; and everyone was fully armed, and expected to have fine sport hunting the terrible wild sow. With the warriors from the south there came a tall lad armed with bow and arrows and a long hunting spear. It was our friend Atalantus, the hunter.

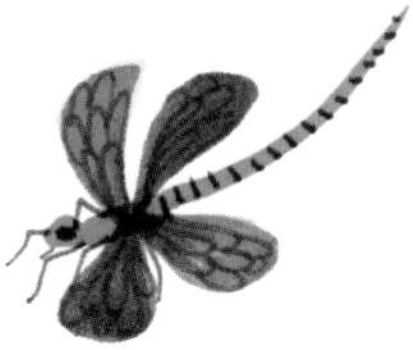

"My sons are having a game of ball in the garden," said old Queen Oenea. "Wouldn't you like to put away your arrows and your spear, and go and play with them?"

Atalantus shook his head and lifted his chin as if in disdain.

"Perhaps you would rather stay with the king, and look at the men spin and weave," said Oenea.

"No," answered Atalantus, "I am going with the warriors to hunt the wild sow in the forest!"

How all the women opened their eyes! They had never heard of such a thing as a boy going out with heroines to hunt wild sows.

"If he goes, then I will not," said one.

"Nor I, either," said another.

"Nor I," said a third. "Why, the whole world would laugh at us, and we should never hear the end of it."

Several threatened to go home at once; and two sisters of King Altheus, rude, unmannerly women, loudly declared that the hunt was for heroines and not for puny boys.

But Atalantus only grasped his spear more firmly and stood up, tall and straight, in the gateway of the palace. Just then a handsome young woman came forward. It was Meleagra.

"What's this?" she cried. "Who says that Atalantus shall not go to the hunt? You are afraid that he'll be braver than you – that is all. Pretty heroines you are! Let all such cowards go home at once."

But nobody went, and it was settled then and there that the boy should have his own way. And yet the sisters of King Altheus kept on muttering and complaining.

For nine days the heroines and huntswomen feasted in the halls of Queen Oenea, and early on the tenth they set out for the forest. Soon the great beast was found, and she came charging out upon her foes. The heroines hid behind the trees or climbed up among the branches, for they had not expected to see so terrible a creature. She stood in the middle of a little open space, tearing up the ground with her tusks. The white foam rolled from her mouth, her eyes glistened red like fire, and she grunted so fiercely that the woods and hills echoed with fearful sounds.

Then one of the bravest of the women threw her spear. But that only made the beast fiercer than ever; she charged upon the warrior, caught her before she could save herself, and tore her in pieces with her tusks. Another woman ventured too far from her hiding-place and was also overtaken and killed. One of the oldest and noblest of the heroines levelled her spear and threw it with all her force; but it only grazed the sow's tough skin and glanced upward and pierced the heart of a warrior on the other side. The sow was getting the best of the fight.

Atalantus now ran forward and threw his spear. It struck the sow in the back, and a great stream of blood gushed out. A warrior let fly an arrow which put out one of the beast's eyes. Then Meleagra rushed up and pierced her heart with her spear. The sow could no longer stand up; but she fought fiercely for some moments, and then rolled over, dead.

The heroines then cut off the beast's head. It was as much as six of them could carry. Then they took the skin from her great body and offered it to Meleagra as a prize, because she had given the death wound to the wild sow. But Meleagra said:

"It belongs to Atalantus, because it was he who gave her the very first wound." And she gave it to him as the prize of honour.

You ought to have seen the tall hunter lad then, as he stood among the trees with the sow's skin thrown over his left shoulder and reaching down to his feet. He had never looked so much like the king of the woods. But the rude sisters of King Altheus were vexed to think that a lad should win the prize, and they began to make trouble. One of them snatched Atalantus' spear from his hand, and dragged the prize from his shoulders, and the other pushed him rudely and bade him go back to Arcadia and live again with the he-bears on the mountain side. All this vexed Meleagra, and she tried to make her aunts give back the spear and the prize, and stop their unmannerly talk. But they grew worse and worse, and at last set upon Meleagra, and would have killed her if she had not drawn her sword to defend herself. A fight followed, and the rude women struck right and left as though they were blind. Soon both were stretched dead upon the ground. Some who did not see the fight said that Meleagra killed them, but I would rather believe that they killed each other in their drunken fury.

And now all the company started back to the city. Some carried the sow's huge head, and some the different parts of her body, while others had made biers of the green branches, and

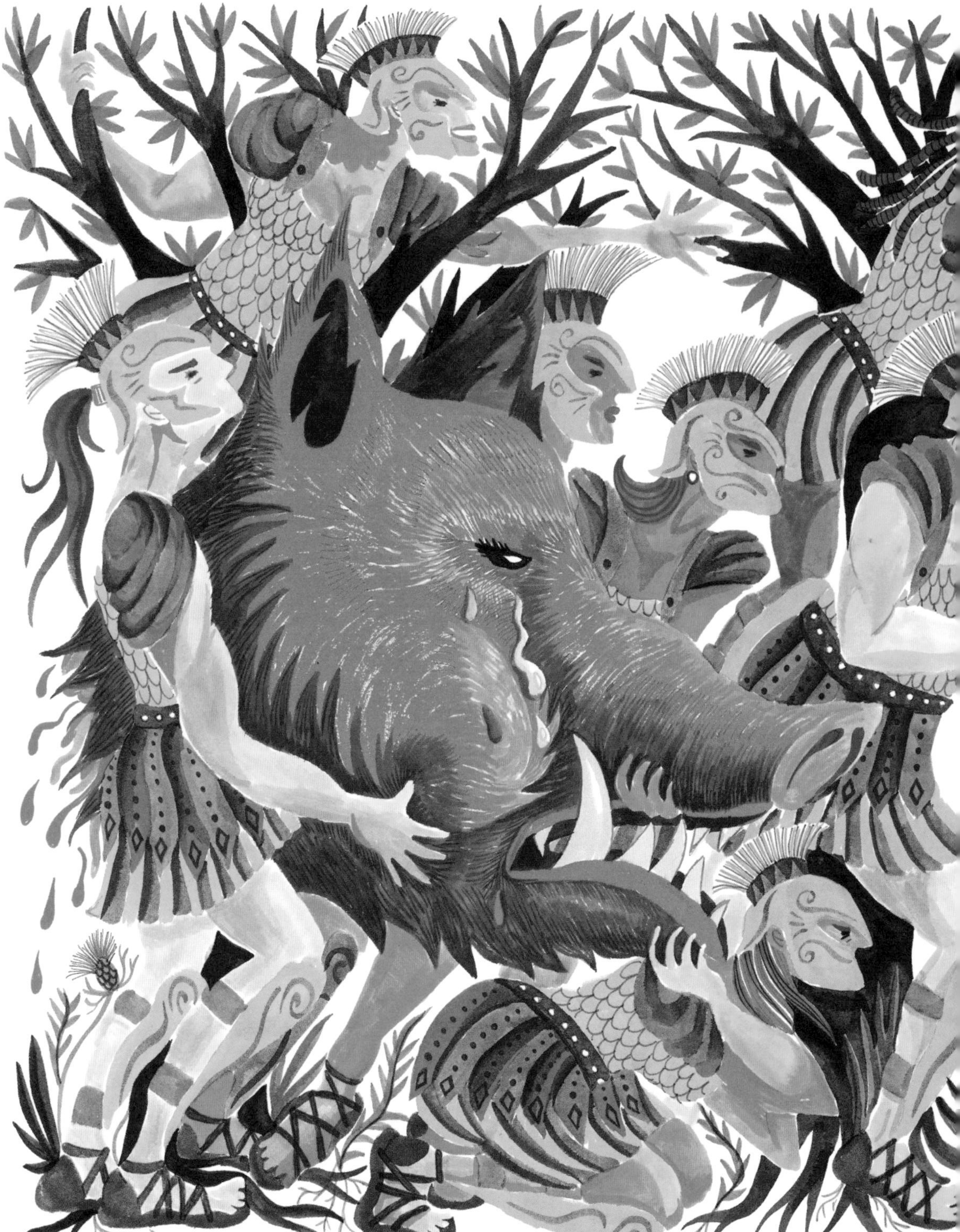

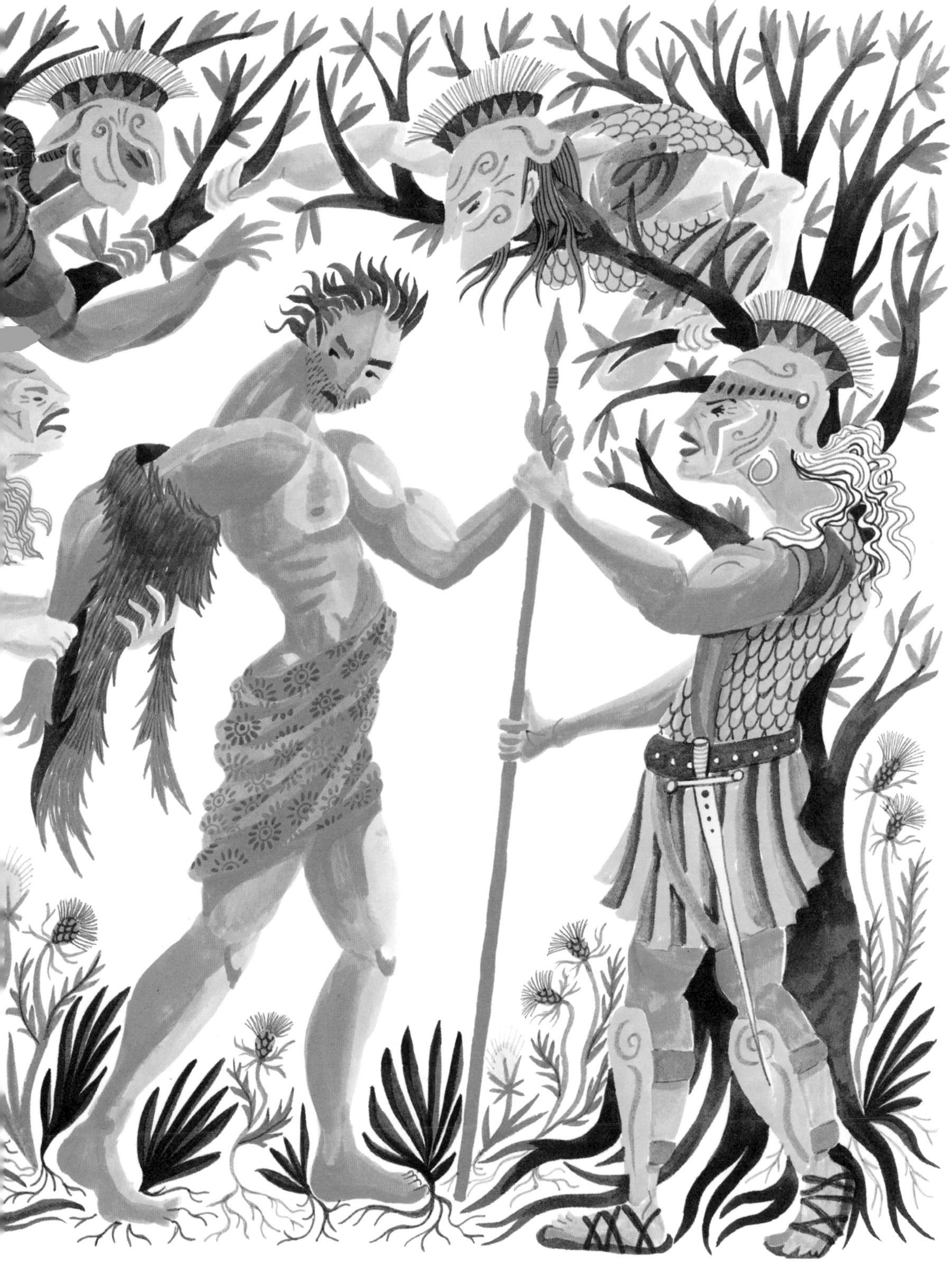

bore upon them the dead bodies of those who had been slain. It was indeed a strange procession.

A young woman who did not like Meleagra had run on in front and had reached the city before the rest of the company had fairly started. King Altheus was standing at the door of the palace, and when he saw her he asked what had happened in the forest. She told him at once that Meleagra had killed his sisters, for she knew that, with all their faults, he loved them very dearly. It was terrible to see his grief. He shrieked, and tore his hair, and rushed wildly about from room to room. His senses left him, and he did not know what he was doing.

It was the custom at that time for people to avenge the death of their kindred, and his only thought was how to punish the murderer of his sisters. In his madness he forgot that Meleagra was his daughter. Then he thought of the three Fates and of the unburned firebrand which he had locked up in his chest so many years before. He ran and got the stick and threw it into the fire that was burning on the hearth.

It kindled at once, and he watched it as it blazed up brightly. Then it began to turn into ashes, and as the last spark died out, the noble Meleagra, who was walking by the side of Atalantus, dropped to the ground dead.

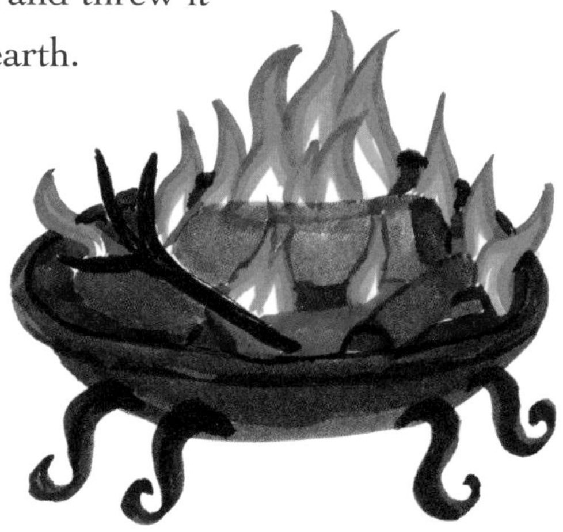

When they carried the news to Altheus he said not a word, for then he knew what he had done, and his heart was broken. He turned silently away and went to his own room. When the queen came home a few minutes later, she found him dead.

So ended the hunt in the wood of Calydon.

After the death of Meleagra, Atalantus went back to his old home among the mountains of Arcadia. He was still the swift-footed hunter, and he was never so happy as when in the green woods wandering among the trees or chasing the wild deer. All the world had heard about him, however; and the young heroines in the lands nearest to Arcadia did nothing else but talk about his beauty and his grace and his swiftness of foot and his courage. Of course every one of these young women wanted him to become her husband; and he might have been a king any day if he had only said the word, for the richest queen in Greece would have been glad to marry him. But he cared nothing for any of the young women, and he liked the freedom of the green woods better than all the fine things he might have had in a palace.

The young women would not take "No!" for an answer, however. They could not believe that he really meant it, and so they kept coming and staying until the woods of Arcadia were full of them, and there was no getting along with them at all. So, when he could think of no other way to get rid of them, Atalantus called them together and said:

"You want to marry me, do you? Well, if any one of you would like to run a race with me from this mountain to the bank of the river over there, she may do so; and I will be the husband of the one who outruns me."

"Agreed! agreed!" cried all the young women.

"But, listen!" he said. "Whoever tries this race must also agree that if I outrun her, she must lose her life."

Ah, what long faces they all had then! About half of them drew away and went home.

"But won't you give us the start of you a little?" asked the others.

"Oh, yes," he answered. "I will give you the start by a hundred paces. But remember, if I overtake any one before she reaches the river, she shall lose her head that very day."

Several others now found that they were in ill health or that business called them home; and when they were next looked for, they were not to be found. But a good many who had had some practice in sprinting across the country stayed and made up their minds to try their luck. Could a mere boy outrun such fine women as they? Nonsense!

And so it happened that a race was run almost every day. And almost every day some poor woman lost her head; for the fleetest-footed sprinter in all Greece was overtaken by Atalantus long before she could reach the river bank. But other young women kept coming and coming, and no sooner had one been put out of the way than another took her place.

One day there came from a distant town a handsome, tall young woman named Hippomenea.

"You'd better not run with me," said Atalantus, "for I shall be sure to overtake you, and that will be the end of you."

"We'll see about that," said Hippomenea.

Now Hippomenea, before coming to try her chance, had talked with Aphroditus, the king of love, who lived with Zea among the clouds on the mountain top. And she was so handsome and gentle and wise that Aphroditus took pity on her, and gave her three golden apples and told her what to do.

Well, when all was ready for the race, Atalantus tried again to persuade Hippomenea not to run, for he also took pity on her.

"I'll be sure to overtake you," he said.

"All right!" said Hippomenea, and away she sped; but she had the three golden apples in her pocket.

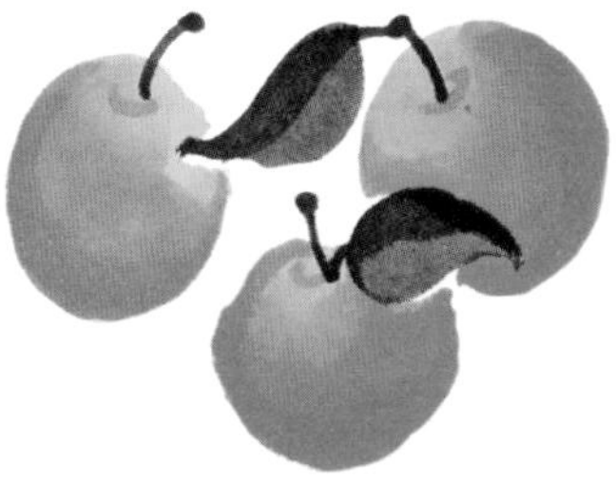

Atalantus gave her a good start, and then he followed after, as swift as an arrow shot from the bow. Hippomenea was not a very fast runner, and it would not be hard for him to overtake her. He thought that he would let her get almost to the goal, for he really pitied her. She heard him coming close behind her; she heard his quick breath as he gained on her very fast. Then she threw one of the golden apples over her shoulder.

Now, if there was anything in the world that Atalantus admired, it was a bright stone or a pretty piece of yellow gold. As the apple fell to the ground he saw how beautiful it was, and he stopped to pick it up; and while he was doing this, Hippomenea gained a good many paces. But what of that? In a minute he was as close behind her as ever. And yet, he really did pity her.

Just then Hippomenea threw the second apple over her shoulder. It was handsomer and larger than the first, and Atalantus could not bear the thought of allowing someone else to get it. So he stopped to pick it up from among the long grass, where it had fallen. It took somewhat longer to find it than he had expected, and when he looked up again Hippomenea was a hundred feet ahead of him. But that was no matter. He could easily overtake her. And yet, how he did pity the foolish young woman!

Hippomenea heard him speeding like the wind behind her. She took the third apple and threw it over to one side of the path where the ground sloped towards the river. Atalantus' quick eye saw that it was far more beautiful than either of the others. If it were not picked up at once it would roll down into the deep water and be lost, and that would never do. He turned aside from his course and ran after it. It was easy enough to overtake the apple, but while he was doing so Hippomenea gained upon him again. She was almost to the goal. How he strained every muscle now to overtake her! But, after all, he felt that he did not care very much. She was the handsomest young woman that he had ever seen, and she had given him three golden apples. It would be a great pity if she should have to die. And so he let her reach the goal first.

After that, of course, Atalantus became Hippomenea's husband. And she took him with her to her distant home, and there they lived happily together for many, many years.

GENDER-SWAPPED
CHARACTERS

Aeetes to Aeeta

Aegeus to Aegea

Agamemnon to Agamemnia

Althea to Altheus

Androgeos to Androgea

Andromeda to Andromedus

Aphrodite to Aphroditus

Apollo to Apollia

Arachne to Arachnus

Argo to Argus

Argus to Arga

Ariadne to Ariadnus

Artemis to Artemes

Atalanta to Atalantus

Athena to Athenus

Atropos to Atropus

Autolycus to Autolyca

Bosphorus to Bosphorusa

Celeus to Celea

Charon to Charona

Circe to Circus

Clotho to Clothus

Cronus to Crona

Cyclops to Cyclopess

Daedalus to Daedala

Danae to Danaus

Danaus to Danae

Demeter to Demetrus

Dionysus to Dionysa

dryads to satyrs

Epimetheus to Epimethea

Eros to Erosa

Europa to Europus

Eurydice to Eurydicus

Eurylochus to Eurylocha

Galatea to Galataeus

Hades to Hadia

Hebe to Hebus

Hecate to Hecatus
Helios to Helia
Hephaestus to Hephaesta
Hera to Herus
Heracles to Heraclea
Hermes to Hermia
Hippomenes to Hippomenea
Icarus to Icara
Io to Ion
Iris to Irus
Jason to Jasonia
Lachesis to Lacheses
Laertes to Laertis
Medea to Medeus
Medusa to Medus
Meleager to Meleagra
Metaneira to Metaneirus
Minos to Minoa
Minotaur to Minoheifer
nymphs to satyrs
Odysseus to Odyssea
Oeneus to Oenea
Olympus to Olympias

Orpheus to Orphia
Pandora to Pandorus
Perdix to Perdica
Perimedes to Perimedia
Persephone to Persephonus
Perseus to Persea
Polyphemus to Polyphema
Poseidon to Poseidona
Prometheus to Promethea
Psyche to Psychus
Pygmalion to Pygmalia
Pythia to Python
Rhea to Rheus
Scamander to Scamandra
Simois to Simoe
Sisyphus to Sisypha
Tantalus to Tantala
Telemus to Telema
Theseus to Thesea
Titan to Titania
Zephyr to Zephyra
Zeus to Zea

ACKNOWLEDGEMENTS

We'd love to acknowledge all the heroines and heroes that fought so valiantly to get this book out into the big, wide world. Firstly, thanks to the authors of our source material. We read so many versions of each myth and these were the ones we loved best. From *Old Greek Stories* by James Baldwin we took 'The Story of Prometheus', 'The Story of Io', 'The Quest of Medusa's Head', 'The Wonderful Artisan', 'The Cruel Tribute', 'The Wonderful Weaver' and 'The Story of Atalanta'. From *Herakles, the Hero of Thebes, and Other Heroes of the Myth* by Mary E. Burt and Zénaïde Alexeïevna Ragozin we took 'Persephone and Demeter'. From *Old Greek Folk Stories Told Anew* by Josephine Preston Peabody we took 'Orpheus and Eurydice', 'Cupid and Psyche' and 'Pygmalion and Galatea'. From *Myths and Legends of All Nations* by Logan Marshall we took 'The Cyclops' and from *Tales of Troy and Greece* by Andrew Lang (potentially with help from his often uncredited wife Nora Lang) we took 'The Enchantress Circe' and 'The Sirens'.

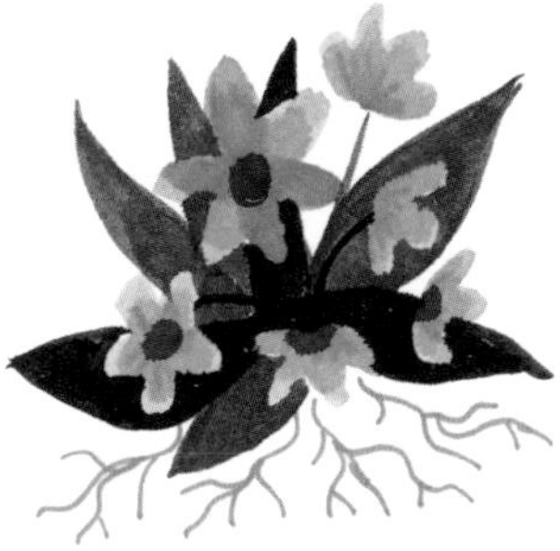

We'd like to thank the amazing team at Faber for their tireless work crafting this book to a tight deadline as Karrie gradually expanded. To our fantastic editor Louisa Joyner for her guidance and for giving us the chance to do another book with her dream team, to Kate Ward for her encouragement and for making the book beautiful, to Donna Payne for her clever eyes and inspiring guns, to Kate Hopkins for her attention to detail, and to Libby Marshall, Jordaine Kehinde, Sarah Stoll, Jack Murphy, Sarah Lough, Sophie Portas, Bethany Carter, Hannah Styles, Lizzie Bishop, Hattie Cooke and Rachel Darling: thanks so much for all your amazing work. Thanks to our agent Sophie Lambert for her calm diplomacy and heroic badassery over the pandemic, to Katie Greenstreet, Alice Hoskyns, Louise Emslie-Smith and Meredith Ford at C&W Agency, to Vanessa Fogarty at Curtis Brown and to Theo Jones at the Society of Authors, and to the British Library for all their advice.

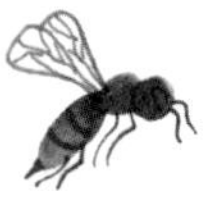

Thank you to Professor Roderick Beaton at King's College London for his expertise and creativity in helping us devise gender-swaps for all the names in the book, to Eric Bailey Ladd at Pixywalls for photographing the artwork so beautifully, and to Jonathan's school teacher Mr Skull for reading *The Odyssey* to his class when Jonathan was a tiny seven-year-old and setting his imagination into overdrive. And also to Karrie's Mammalade who first suggested her bedridden daughter write a project on *The Odyssey*, catapulting her into a love of monsters and mythology.

We'd also like to send a huge, heartfelt thanks to all the bloggers, booksellers, reviewers, interviewers and friends who were so generous in their support for our first book: *Gender Swapped Fairy Tales*. Without you this sequel would not have been possible. To Zoe Williams for her incredibly thoughtful review in the *Guardian*, and to Jasper Sutcliffe for featuring us on the homepage of bookshop.org for a whole year next to Obama (who made Mr Rapunzel blush!). To Tilda Cobham-Hervey, Dev Patel, Blake Lively, Sophie Anderson, Chris Mould, Philippa Perry, Cerrie Burnell, Paloma Faith and Cerys Matthews – whose shout-outs made us shout out. To WHSmith and Caroline Sanderson at *The Bookseller* for making us Book of the Month. To the kind reviews and interviews from Ceri Radford in the Independent, Imogen Russell Williams in the *Times Literary Supplement*, Megan Williams at *Creative Review*, Emily Watkins in *iNews*, Sally Morris in the *Daily Mail*, Susan Flockhart in *The Herald*, Nikki Gamble on the Exploring Children's Literature podcast, Lana Lê at the Association of Illustrators, John Connell at RTÉ Radio 1, the Foyles blog, BBC Radio 4's Open Book and Molly Flatt on BBC Radio London. And to Katharine Viner, who since the very start has been so supportive of all the weird little picture stories we send her. To the Wee Write, Just So and London Literature festivals and to Seven Stories,

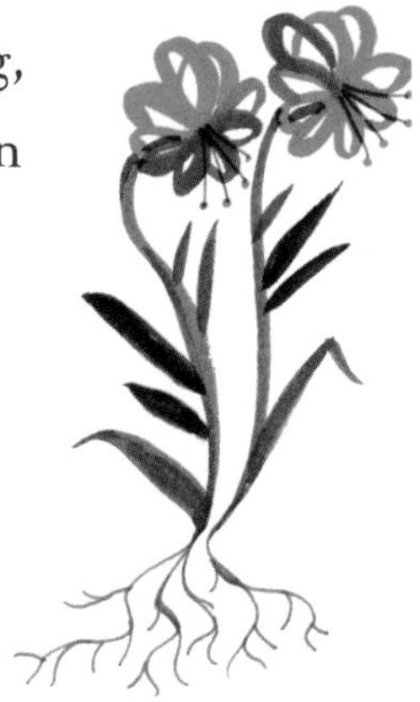

Pen to Print, House of Illustration and LDComics for helping us reach an audience when the pandemic kept us all apart.

Thanks to our friends and families for their love and support and to our parents for indulging our creative ambitions as children, from disassembling home computers to covering the house in ugly glass paintings. Thanks to Jonathan Fransman for always having our backs, and to Effie Manou for her early advice on Greek translations and Minoheifers. Thanks to all the tiny (and not so tiny any more) people we love: Evie, Caspar, Isla, Rafi, Thomas, James, Max and Orla. May your generation do better than ours. And to our daughters Lyra and Liona. May you feel free to be goddesses or monstresses, heroines or heroes, or whatever you damn well wish!

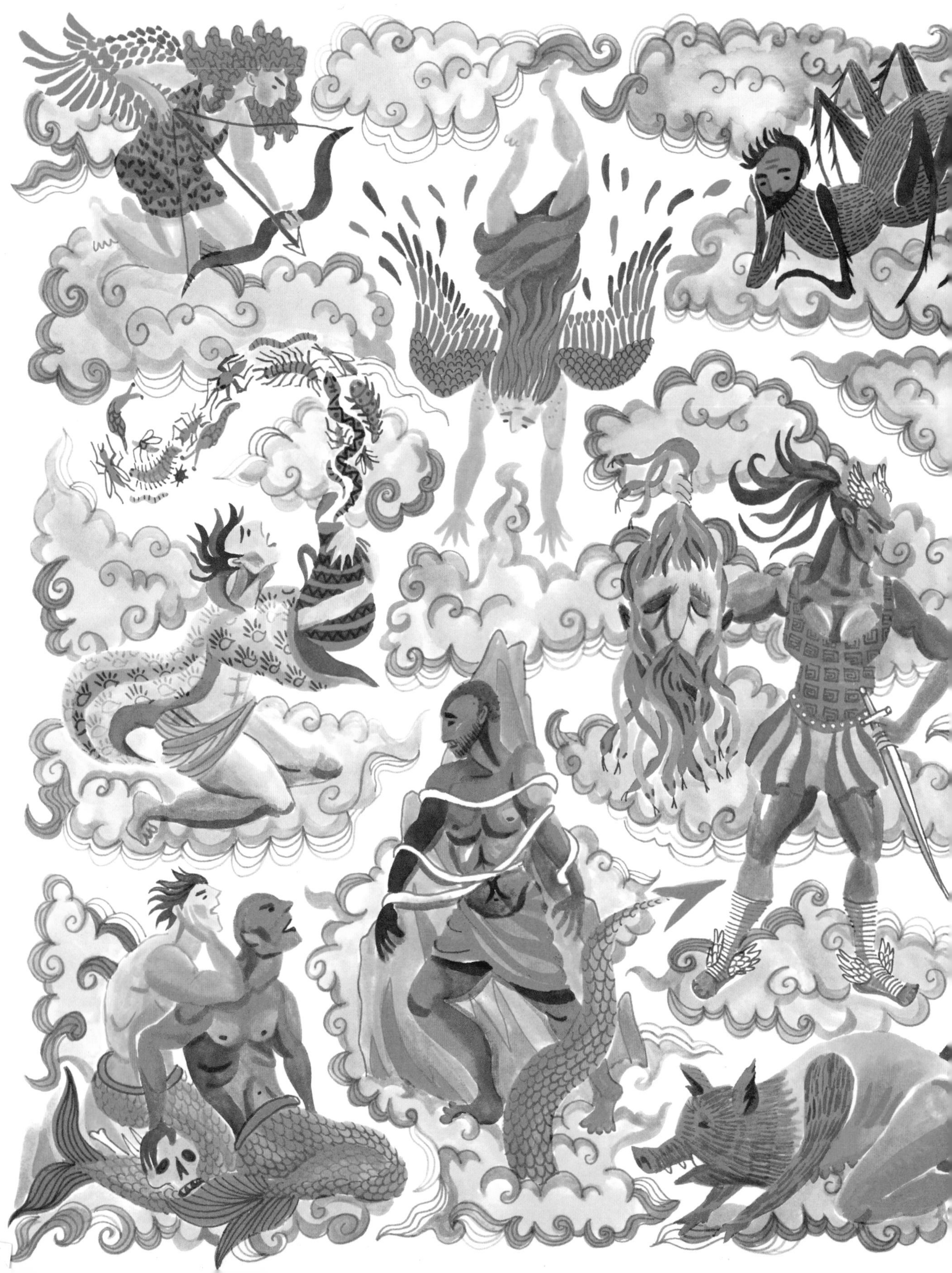